HATE THE WAY HE LOVES ME

STACEY COVINGTON-LEE

Copyright © 2014 Stacey Covington-Lee.

All Rights Reserved

This is a work of fiction and is not meant to depict, portray, or represent any particular person. Names, characters, places, and incidents are either the product of the author's imagination or are used fictionally. Any resemblances to an actual person, living or dead, is entirely coincidental.

All rights reserved. No part of this publication may be reproduced, stored in, or introduced into any retrieval system or transmitted in any form or by any means (electronic mechanical, photocopying, recording, or otherwise) without written permission of the copyright owner.

Cover Design: The Final Wrap

Formatting/Typesetting: Under Cover Designs

ISBN – 978-1-7338811-3-5

Second Printing @ Copyright 2019

Published by SCL Novel Publications

Printed in the United States of America

This is for my "Ride or Die" Cassandra Smith. You encouraged all of this and I am forever grateful to you. I love you and you shall always remain in my heart.

CHAPTER ONE

Exhausted, Zoe fell into bed at 11:00pm with high hopes of a long, peaceful slumber. But by 3:30am, she was tossing, turning, and grunting in her sleep. The disturbing dream quickly turned into a nightmare that had Zoe screaming and swinging at the man that haunted her dreams almost every night. With her arms flailing about, Zoe hit the headboard with her hand and the pain that it caused jolted her back to full consciousness. She sat up in bed with sweat running down her face. Looking around, she realized that she was alone in the sanctity of her home. Wiping her face, Zoe cursed her father for once again ruining what was to be a perfect night's rest. Hoping that she'd at least made it through most of the night, she turned to check the time and became further disgusted once she realized how many hours lay ahead of her before the alarm clock would sound.

"Damn it, is eight hours of sleep really too much to ask for?" Zoe mumbled as she threw her legs over the side of the bed, slipped on her house shoes and padded down the hall towards the kitchen. She snatched the tea kettle off of the stove and filled it with water. While it began to heat, she retrieved the hot chocolate from the pantry. Short of prescribed medication, this was the only thing that soothed her nerves and allowed her to relax enough to drift back off to sleep.

With so many nightmares, she had officially become a hot chocolate addict, but that was better than becoming a real addict. She'd been given prescription after prescription for everything from insomnia to depression. Neither of the diagnoses' was a problem for her, but the doctor's didn't seem to comprehend what the real issue was. They were content to slap a band aid on the gaping wound that plagued Zoe nightly. Two cups of cocoa and an hour later, Zoe drifted back off to sleep.

Ring…ring…ring… It wasn't the alarm clock, but the incessant noise from the telephone that woke Zoe. "Crap, I'm late," she declared as she jumped up and ran for the bathroom. Whoever was calling would have to wait.

A quick shower, a little mascara and Zoe was out the door. The bank would open in twenty minutes and she hadn't even distributed money to each of her tellers for their cash drawers. She called Cathy, her best teller, and asked her to get things started for her. She breezed through town and was at work in ten minutes flat. One of the few benefits of living in a small town was the lack of traffic. Unfortunately, Susan, the branch manager, was the one to open the door for her.

"Sorry I'm running late. I'll have everything set up in five minutes."

"You were promoted to Head Teller because we thought that you were responsible and could successfully handle everything that the position entails. You can't handle it if you're not here, Zoe."

"I also can't handle it if you keep me from my work with your lecture." Zoe rolled her eyes and strutted off as she mumbled under her breath, "I can't wait to get away from her." She hustled to the vault to retrieve the money for her drawer, double checked the other teller's cash drawers to make sure that Cathy had done everything correctly, and was ready to serve customers once the doors were opened for business. Her very first customer of the day was a short, stubby man with an out of control beard.

"Good morning, sir, how may I help you?"

"Give me all of the money out of each teller's drawer and do not trip the alarm or give me a dye pack. If you do, I swear I'll come back here and blow your brains out." He discreetly displayed a small caliber gun and passed Zoe a cloth bag for the money.

Without fear, Zoe tripped the alarm and gave him the dye pack. She watched him walk out the door as if he'd just pulled off the most successful bank heist ever. She immediately ran to the front door and turned the lock. "I swear I'm surrounded by dumb ass people. It is definitely time for me to get out of dodge," she declared.

CHAPTER TWO

Pulling up to her driveway, Zoe saw that her mom and sister were already waiting on her front porch. She figured they'd seen the news report about the bank robbery and while she was not really in the mood to talk about it, she loved the fact that she could always depend on the two of them for emotional support. Zoe killed the car's engine, took a deep breath and reached for the door handle. But before she could get a good grasp of it, Pamela snatched the door open. Zoe could always depend on her sister to bring the drama.

"Oh my gosh Zoe, are you okay? We saw the news and I swear I've been a shaking ball of nerves ever since. Come on now, step out of the car; let me see you so I know for sure that you're okay." Pam turned Zoe from side to side as if she were inspecting her for bullet wounds. "Thank God that you weren't hurt, at least you don't look like you were."

"For the love of God, Pam, move out of her way so that the child can go in the house," Martha instructed. She pulled Pam to the side and watched as her baby girl gathered her things from the car and made her way to the front door. Martha waddled in the door behind Zoe and Pam followed closely behind them both, locking the door and rechecking the lock to make sure that it was secure. Zoe dropped her things on the table, but before she could plop down in one of her chairs, Martha grabbed her and pulled her close. She held Zoe and rocked her from side to side as tears flowed down her face.

"Mama, it's okay, I'm fine. I promise. No one was hurt. I gave him the money, he left the bank, and I ran and locked the door behind him. The cops were there in no time and right before I left they informed us that they'd caught the guy."

"We've been through so much already, I hate that you now have to deal with the possibility of some desperate fool threatening your life." Martha sobbed and continued to hold onto Zoe as if her arms could shield her from any further hurt, harm or danger. But all three of the ladies knew that Martha had never been able to protect them when they needed it most.

"Mama, come on now, stop that crying and sit down. I'll fix us some tea and we can focus on something a little more positive rather than that stupid robbery. Don't you want some tea?"

"Yes, baby, tea would be nice, but let me fix it for you. Have a seat, Pamela and I will fix the tea and a nice meal to go along with it. Won't we Pam?"

"Of course we will. Let me check the locks to make sure that they're good and secure." Zoe and Martha watched as Pam checked each door lock once, twice, and then a third time. "Okay Mama, what are we going to fix for dinner?"

Zoe watched as her mother rummaged through the refrigerator and pantry for the makings of a good meal. Her heart sank a little bit as she took notice of the additional weight her mother had gained. At two hundred twenty-five pounds, Zoe didn't know how much more weight her five foot two inch frame could handle before something went seriously wrong. She glanced at her older sister walking back and forth from the sink to the door, checking the locks over and over again. Zoe took a deep breath, shook her head and decided to head down the hall and get out of her work clothes. She was mentally drained and wanted nothing more than a good night's sleep. But as she stepped into her bedroom, the four poster oak queen bed seemed to taunt her. It was as if she could hear it whisper, *come on, dear, I've got a nightmare waiting for you.* Disgusted, Zoe snatched off her clothes, pulled on some sweats and headed back down the hall.

It didn't take Martha long to throw together a meal of fried chicken, mac and cheese, green beans, and corn bread. Zoe would've been completely satisfied with a small tossed salad, but her mom didn't consider that real food. Zoe sat down and watched as Pam filled three glasses with tea and her mom heaped food upon her Walmart plates.

"Everything looks good, Mama, but I'm not all that hungry. You can take some of that food off of my plate. That way I'll have some left over for my dinner tomorrow."

"Non sense young lady. You can eat all of this and still have plenty left over," Martha grunted as she plopped down in her chair. She reached for her daughters' hands, bowed her head, and led them in prayer. "Eat up now. I know that it's not often that y'all eat like this. You both have gotten all healthy on me. Don't want to eat fried foods or any of that good stuff I used to make for us, but you both can make an exception today."

"Of course we'll make the exception for this, Mama, it's all delicious," Pam declared. Zoe agreed and both the sisters stuffed themselves for the sake of saving their mother's feelings.

"I have some news for you Zoe," Martha spoke timidly, like she was afraid to speak the words that she knew would weigh heavy on the three of them. Pam had already begun to cry, not her usual theatrical tears, but real tears filled with fear.

"What is it Mama? Did someone die?"

"No, baby, thank God we haven't lost anyone, but this…this is what we've feared for a very long time."

"Otis?" Zoe quizzed with a twisted mouth as if speaking her father's name left a foul taste on her tongue.

"Yes. I got this letter from the District Attorney's office saying that the parole board decided to set him free. They feel that he has been rehabilitated and can now be a positive contributor to society."

She held the letter in her trembling hand and though she tried to appear unfazed, the truth was written all over her face and her eyes puddled with fear.

Zoe snatched the letter and read it three times before she looked back up into the faces that were staring at her. They were waiting for her, the baby of the family, to provide the plan for how they would handle this threat to their lives.

"I can't believe that this animal convinced an entire board of folks that he was fit to live among the general public. That board must be comprised of fools."

Zoe's mind was spinning; she knew that action would have to be taken to keep her father from finding them. After his conviction, Zoe had moved them all to Manassas, Virginia and they'd been living an easy, peaceful life ever since. They assumed he'd never get out of prison and that no one from his side of the family knew where they'd disappeared to. But low and behold, three years after relocating, her father's sister managed to track them down. And now this. They all knew that within two weeks of his release he'd appear in their small town and shatter the sense of peace they'd been so comfortable with.

Wringing her hands nervously, Pam timidly asked, "What are we going to do, Zoe?"

"I don't know!" Zoe snapped. She instantly regretted her angry, harsh tone. The tears that now flowed a little more freely down Pam's face were a clear indication that her sister was hurt and confused. "I'm sorry Pam. I didn't mean to snap at you. I'm just so upset and confused by this decision, but I shouldn't have spoken to you like that. I apologize, honey." Zoe always tried to be very careful of how she dealt with Pam. After all that Otis had put her through, Pam was fragile and often needed to be handled with kid gloves.

"It's okay; I know you didn't mean it, we're all upset and on edge. I guess I'm just anxious to know what our next move will be, how we will protect ourselves."

Zoe knew full well what her sister was really asking was how she would protect them. "Guys, you know I love you and you know that I'll figure something out. Give me a little time to think through this and I'll let you know what our game plan is, okay?"

Confident in Zoe's strength and resourcefulness, Martha and Pam made their exit and would patiently wait for direction from their fearless leader.

CHAPTER THREE

Despite all of the thoughts that were running through her head and the heaviness she held in her chest, exhaustion overtook her and Zoe fell into a deep slumber. She was having the sweetest dream where she, her mother, and sister were in their old home, laughing, and baking cookies. Martha was sharing stories from her childhood while she and Pam eased chocolate chips from the counter and popped them into their mouths. As they were all using their sticky fingers to drop dollops of cookie dough onto the metal sheet, they heard the front door slam. Instantly, all of the joy was sucked out of the room and replaced with fear. Otis stumbled into the kitchen, looked at Martha with bloodshot eyes and started in.

"What the fuck you bitches doing?"

"Daddy, we're baking cookies. See, doesn't the batter look good? Do you want to taste?" Pam asked with a smile on her face and a tremble in her voice.

"Do I look like I want to taste some damn raw cookies?" Otis yelled as he snatched the pan of cookie dough from his oldest daughter's hands. He threw the batter at Pam and when he'd flung the last plop of it, he began to beat her about the head with the pan. "You have got to be the dumbest bitch ever born," he spat as he hit her over and over again. "I told your sorry ass mama to have an abortion, but no, she had your dumb ass." Whack... "You stupid bitch." Whack... "You sorry whore." Whack... "I hate you!" Whack...

Martha grabbed his arm, "Stop it, Otis, you're drunk. Leave her alone."

Without hesitation, Otis turned his anger on Martha and struck her across her face with his open hand. "Bitch, did I tell you to touch me? Don't you ever put your hands on me!" He drew his hand back and broke Martha's nose with one punch of his now closed fist. As blood spewed from her nose, Otis yelled, "Bitch, your fat ass better stop bleeding on my damn floor." Martha held her face and screamed in pain which only angered him more. He grabbed her by the hair and slammed her head into the cabinet, "Shut the fuck up and stop bleeding."

Zoe cowered in the corner as she watched her father turn his attention back to Pam. "You want to give me something, girl? Come on, I know what you can give me."

He grabbed her by the arm and dragged her down the hall as she kicked and screamed. Martha took off running behind them, but Otis slammed the door in her face and locked it. All Martha could do was weep at the door as her daughter cried out and begged for help. Otis was stinking drunk which meant he took even longer to finish his business. Zoe cried for her sister and covered her ears to try and mute the pleas for mercy. Finally the screams stopped and the door opened. Otis stumbled out and Martha ran in to try and comfort her baby. As Otis headed out of the door, he looked at Zoe still cowering in the corner and warned, "You're next, baby girl."

The blaring alarm clock jolted Zoe from the horrific dream. She sat up and wept as she realized that the dream was actually one of the many memories that she'd unsuccessfully tried to bury. Otis was like a savage beast that had been turned loose on them. It took years for him to be caught and caged and Zoe cried uncontrollably at the thought of him being unleashed on them again. They only had two months before he would walk out of prison a free man. She had to devise a plan and implement it quickly.

Driving in to work, Zoe decided to call her best friend, Desmond. They'd grown up together in DC and supported one another in a way that no one else had been able to. His house was her hide out when she needed to stay out of Otis' path and her shoulder was the one he'd cried on when neighborhood kids tormented him for being gay. Early on they developed a mutual love and respect for one another, a bond that remained unbreakable. Even though Desmond decided to move to Atlanta in search of a better life and more acceptance, they still spoke daily, serving as one another's sounding board for whatever issues might arise.

Finally after several rings, Desmond picked up. "Girl, what you doing calling me this early? You know I don't speak or move before 10:00am."

"Boy, can't you just say hello like normal people?"

"Not before 10:00 I can't. Now tell your man what's going on because you never call me this early unless there's a problem."

"They're letting Otis out," Zoe said bluntly.

"Zoe, that's not funny and it's too early to be playing."

"I'm not playing, Desi, they're really going to let him out."

"I can't believe it; after all he did to you and your family they're really going to set him free." Desmond sat up in bed, now fully awake and thinking of the horror that this could mean for his beloved Zoe. "Did they give you guys a chance to speak out against him at the parole hearing?"

"Yep and we were there front and center. We told them how he beat Mom and all the sick ways he tortured Pam, but apparently it was all in vain. In two months he'll be walking the streets and I'm sure that by now he knows where we've relocated to."

"So what are y'all going to do? You *can't* stay there, that fool will be on your doorstep within a week of his release."

"I don't know yet. The bank has branches in Virginia Beach, maybe we'll go there."

"No, come here." Desmond suggested.

"Desi, I don't know anyone in Atlanta and my bank does not have locations in Georgia. Remember, I'll be the sole supporter of us all for the first few months. Mom will probably find work within a month or two, but it always takes Pam longer. Hell, we'll be in our new place six months before she'll feel comfortable going out alone."

"Zoe, you know me and I have made a lot of connections. As a matter of fact, I'm pretty cool with this guy that holds a high position at Citizen's Bank. Send me your resume today, I'll talk to him and put in a good word for you."

"Wow, Desi, Atlanta is such a long way away. We'll be cutting ties with everything and everyone we've ever known. That is going to be a major, and I mean a *major* adjustment for Pam."

"Would you rather have her make the difficult adjustment or be attacked by Otis again?"

The realization of what Desmond said hit Zoe like a ton of bricks. She'd vowed years ago that Otis would never hurt any of them ever again. "You'll have my resume by the end of the day and I'll give serious consideration to your suggestion, Desi. I'll call you tomorrow, okay? "

"Alright, sweetheart, I'll talk to you tomorrow, but please think about coming down here. I really think it would be best."

"I will," Zoe assured him and then disconnected the call.

She parked the car in front of the bank and took a few deep breaths in an effort to prepare herself mentally for another days work. She walked in the front door and the rest of the day was a blur. She didn't remember engaging in any conversations with her coworkers, couldn't remember the face of not one of the customers she waited on. Her mind was all consumed with thoughts of Otis and what she should do to keep her mom and sister safe. She'd come to love a lot about Manassas. It was a friendly, peaceful place to live. The only downside to it was her boss, Susan, who was simply an unpleasant person. When she first said that she couldn't wait to get away from Susan, she thought that she might be relocating to another branch on the other side of town. She didn't imagine she'd be considering leaving the entire state of Virginia.

After eating a little of her mom's leftovers and researching landmarks, housing options, and jobs in the Atlanta area, Zoe decided to jump in a hot shower and watch television in bed. She tuned in to a new show about Atlanta's hip hop scene. She didn't know what to think of the women that put up with all of the shenanigans from the men. She was stunned that no one seemed to have the ability to complete a sentence without dropping the "F" bomb, but she had to admit that it was an entertaining show. Not necessarily a good show, just entertaining. She adjusted her pillows and tried to fight against the heaviness of her eyelids. The heaviness won and Zoe drifted off to a restless sleep. She tossed as she dreamt of Otis beating her mother. She moaned as visions of him spitting on Pam danced in her head. She cried as she saw him turn his attention to her. "It's your turn, baby girl," he slurred as he reached for her. Her mother and sister tried to protect her, but Otis locked her in the room and began to tear at her clothes. She fought against him, but he smacked her across the face and threw her down on her twin bed. As he hovered over her and unbuckled his belt, Zoe reached to the night table for her porcelain piggy bank and brought it down with all her might across the side of Otis' head. She screamed as she hit him in the head with the remaining piece of porcelain over and over again. When her arm was too tired to lift again, she dropped the porcelain and screamed for her mother as if she were some kind of wounded wild animal. The screams pierced the quiet of the night and woke her from her nightmare. Again she sat in the middle of her bed, sweating and heaving over the memories that wouldn't stay buried.

It was 4:30am and Zoe found herself sitting at her computer sending Desmond her resume. The decision had been made; the three Shaw women would be packed and gone within a month.

CHAPTER FOUR

Pam cried like a baby when Zoe broke the news that they were moving. Pam had grown comfortable with her surroundings and the people in her small circle. The thought of starting over all but paralyzed her with fear. But she knew that she would have to trust Zoe's decision and be ready to leave the place she'd called home for the past ten years in just a matter of weeks.

Martha was more matter-of-fact about it all. She asked when they were leaving, how much they could take with them, and if they already had a place to stay. She notified her job, pulled all of the money from her profit sharing account, and went about the business of packing up her home. Martha showed very little emotion, she knew that Pam was emotional enough for the both of them. She packed her things as well as Pam's. At this point, all Pam was fully capable of doing was securing the door and window locks over and over again. This was her coping mechanism, what she always did whenever she was scared or nervous.

Susan was sympathetic and very understanding when Zoe explained her situation. She even forwarded Zoe's resume to a friend of hers that was a branch manager for an Atlanta based credit union. But what shocked Zoe the most was that Susan immediately laid her off. Susan was faced with letting one of her employees go anyway due to budget cuts and it only made sense to her to give Zoe the ax. That way, Zoe could go and apply for unemployment benefits before she left town and it would help provide a little financial cushion until new employment could be established.

Over the next couple of weeks, Zoe was able to pin point an area of town that Desmond confirmed was pretty decent. She shopped apartments in the area on the internet and was able to secure a place to live. It was convenient to downtown, had great shopping, and best of all it was within walking distance to Desmond. She contacted all of the utility companies to set up service and confirmed her U Haul rental. With the most important business handled, Zoe began to pack all of her things. She'd always tried not to become too attached to her home, her surroundings. But despite her efforts, she'd grown incredibly attached. Zoe loved the quaint house that she'd been renting for what seemed like forever. She loved and respected her neighbors and couldn't help but to drop a few tears as she placed her personal effects into cardboard boxes. As she wrapped her fragile items and reminisced about her life in Manassas, the phone rang, interrupting her trip down memory lane.

"Hello?"

"Hey, baby girl, please don't hang up. Your aunt told me where you were and was able to get me your number. I'm getting out soon and I just wanted to assure you that I'm a changed man. I know that everything I did to you, your mom, and sister was wrong and I take complete responsibility for it. I would love to see you once I'm released and beg your forgiveness."

"Go to hell!" Zoe slammed down the phone and yanked the cord out of the wall.

He hadn't even been released yet and already Otis was starting his campaign to weasel his way back into her life. At that moment all Zoe could think was 'to hell with memories, we've got to get the hell out of dodge.' Zoe began throwing things in the boxes as if she didn't have another second to spare. She grabbed her cell phone and called her mom.

"Hey, baby."

"Hey Mom, don't tell Pam, but I just got a call from Otis. He wants to see us and beg our forgiveness. I expect that he'll be here on one of our doorsteps within the next few days. We can't be here. I need you to pack a little faster, we're leaving tomorrow night."

"We'll be ready," Martha confirmed.

Her tone was flat and dry. All anyone had to do was mention Otis' name and Martha turned ice cold, no emotion, no warmth. He'd beat all of the love out of her, destroyed her sense of security, and had broken those that she cared for the most… her girls. She said a long time ago that she'd never be able to forgive him, that hatred would always be the dominant emotion where he was concerned.

Within twenty-four hours, Zoe's hired help had hitched her car to the U Haul, packed up her, Pam, and her mom's belongings and they were on the road to Atlanta. Zoe knew that this was the best possible thing for them and she was no longer nervous or anxious about the move. Pam, however, was a train wreck. Tears flowed freely down her face and she was constantly wringing her hands. Zoe reached into her purse and gave poor Pam one of her prescribed anti-anxiety pills. Pam took it with a sip of water and within fifteen minutes, she was calm and relaxed. Unfortunately there was no pill that her mother had been prescribed so she calmed her nerves with food. Sadly, that was Martha's coping mechanism, she ate until she felt better and her girls were scared that she'd eat herself into an early grave.

By 6:00am Zoe was watching the sunrise as they crossed the Georgia border. A sense of peace washed over her and she knew that everything was going to be alright. They would make new lives for themselves and they would thrive, even Pam. Zoe recognized that this was the kind of peace that only God was capable of providing and she thanked Him for it.

Remarkably, the three Shaw women adjusted to their new city relatively quickly. Zoe secured a customer service position with the credit union. Martha fell right into her role as a Pre-K teacher with an elite school and Pam, well it took her a little longer, but she eventually took a secretarial position at a very small accounting firm. Life was good.

CHAPTER FIVE

Desmond sat in his car outside of the credit union waiting for Zoe to get off work. He'd gotten a few suspicious looks from the security guard, but he didn't care what the Barney Fife type officer thought he was up to, he wasn't leaving until he'd coerced Zoe into hanging out with him for a while. Since moving to Atlanta, Zoe had confined all of her activities to work and home. She'd not yet taken the opportunity to do any real site seeing and she definitely hadn't enjoyed one second of the night life.

Finally, after a thirty-five minute wait, Desmond saw his best friend emerge from the bank. As she approached her car, a big smile began to spread across her face. The vision of Desmond leaning against the car with his arms crossed was truly a welcomed sight.

"Desi, what are you doing here?" Zoe quizzed as she wrapped him in a loving embrace.

"I came to take my best girl out to dinner."

"Oh, Desi, you are so sweet and thoughtful, but you know I've got to get home to Mama and Pam. Pam starts freaking out if I'm five minutes late. Besides, I promised them that I'd pick up dinner on my way in."

"Zoe, they are grown ass women, let them get their own

dinner. I mean what was the point in y'all getting the other car if you're still going to have to be the family taxi?"

"Come on now, you know how Pam is. She's still adjusting, we haven't found a therapist that she's happy with yet and my being around seems to make her feel safe."

"Zoe, it's been four months, she's tried six therapists and it's not fair for you to sacrifice your life for your sister. Hell, it's not even fair that she would ask that of you," Desmond huffed as he felt himself becoming more annoyed by the second.

"She didn't ask me to sacrifice my life, Desi; I just know that she needs me." But truth be told, Zoe really did long for a little time away from her family. She loved them dearly, but carrying them emotionally was starting to take a toll on her.

"Get in the car Zoe," Desi demanded. "You can't take care of everyone else if you don't first take care of yourself. Now get in the car, you can call your mom on the way to the restaurant and I promise to bring you back to your car after dinner."

"But I just told you…"

"Get in and let's go. I'm not taking no for an answer." Desmond smiled as he watched Zoe slide into the passenger seat of his car. He took the scenic route from the credit union to the Lenox area in an effort to let Zoe see more of the city. He admired her so much, her strength, resilience, and determination, but he hated that Zoe was willing to put her life on hold for the sake of her family.

The popular hangout was starting to fill quickly with those seeking to release a little stress after a long day's work. Zoe was looking all around, taking in the scenery, and listening to the music that added to the lively atmosphere. As the hostess led them to their table, Zoe also observed the many handsome men that were hanging out. Zoe was a beautiful woman with an hourglass figure and could no doubt have any man that she wanted, but her policy had always been look but don't touch. After all these years, Desi was still the only man that Zoe trusted to not hurt her.

After only one sip of the Pomegranate Martini Desi ordered for her, Zoe felt herself relaxing more than she had in the past six months. By the time the drink was finished, she'd completely forgotten all of her problems and was consumed by the conversation and laughter that she was sharing with her lifelong friend.

"Thank you, Desi, I'm really glad that you took me hostage," Zoe giggled.

"Don't thank me yet. Let's wait and see if you're still appreciative after you've been kidnapped a few more times. Now tell me, are there any fine men at that credit union of yours?"

"Oh please, Desi, Kirk would kick your butt if you even thought about looking at another man. Not to mention the fact that you love him too much to entertain the idea of seeing anyone else."

"I don't know. Things have been really strained between us lately. He seems to be having trust issues all of a sudden and it's about to drive me crazy. I love him, but I don't know how much longer I can live with his speculation and false allegations. It's just ridiculous."

"Okay, where is all this suspicion coming from? I've never known Kirk to be the jealous type. Did you do something, Desi?" Zoe inquired with a sideways glance.

"I didn't do anything. However, when we were out last month, someone I used to date came up to our table and started chatting away. He gave me his card before walking away and now Kirk is convinced that I'm seeing the dude."

"And that's it, nothing else happened?"

"No...well, I mean he did find the card on my desk and got pissed that I hadn't thrown it away and just as I'd convinced him that it was an oversight, the dude called my phone. That sent Kirk into the stratosphere because now he knew that I'd spoken with the guy and gave him my number. I hate being caught in a lie."

"Desi, are you cheating on Kirk? Because I've got to tell you, that would raise all kinds of suspicion with me as well. Why did you feel the need to lie?"

"No, I'm not cheating and I only lied because I know how Kirk can blow innocent stuff out of proportion. The guy now has a new lover of his own and wanted to know if I was still in real estate because they're looking to buy a house. I told him that I wasn't but I knew someone that was a great agent. I didn't have the agent's number available at the time so he was simply calling me back to get the number."

"That's a simple enough explanation, did you tell all of that to Kirk? I mean he is a rational man, no reason he shouldn't believe you."

"Of course I told him, but it meant nothing. He's created some sorted affair in his head and like a dog with a bone, he won't let it go. He's wearing me out and frankly I'm getting tired of it. If he's going to keep accusing me, I may as well be cheating for real."

"No you shouldn't. Just give him a little time; he'll come to realize that you're an innocent man," Zoe assured.

"Well enough about my love life, let's talk about yours," Desi grinned.

"I see you've got jokes cause we all know that I wouldn't know a love life if it jumped up and smacked me in the face,"

"Aren't you ready to change that? Zoe, you are a beautiful woman with so much to offer. Don't you want to share your life with someone other than your mother and sister? I mean don't you want the comfort and love of a man?"

"For the longest time I didn't think that I was relationship material. But truth be told, Desi, I think that I would really enjoy being in a relationship right now. I've been emotionally supporting my family for so long that I feel drained. I would love to know what it's like to have someone be there for me, to emotionally support me, to put my feelings ahead of their own. I want someone to hold me and tell me that everything is going to be alright."

Zoe spoke through tear filled eyes and it was clear to see that she was weak from carrying the load of her and her family's unfortunate drama for so long. Desi moved his chair closer to hers and wrapped her in his arms. And for the first time in a long time, right there in the middle of the restaurant, Zoe allowed a river of tears to flow freely. She sobbed quietly for what seemed like forever, but in reality was only for a few minutes. When she finally raised her head from Desi's shoulder and began to dry her eyes, she was embarrassed to see a tall, handsome, well groomed man watching her. She quickly averted her eyes and continued her conversation with Desi.

Zoe heard her cell phone ringing for the fifth time tonight and decided that she could no longer ignore it. She swiped her finger across the screen, took a deep breath and answered.

"Hello?"

"Zoe, are you okay? I've been calling you, when are you coming home?" Pam sounded almost hysterical.

"Didn't Mom tell you that I was going out to dinner with Desi?"

"Well yes, but I thought you would've been home by now."

"Pam, I just left work two hours ago and you know it. I will be leaving shortly and heading home, but in the meantime don't call me again unless it's an emergency. Do you understand?"

"You don't have to talk to me like I'm a child."

"Then stop acting like one, Pam. Be the strong woman that I know you are."

"Okay and I'm sorry for disturbing your evening out. I'll see you when you get home. And Zoe…I love you."

"I love you too, Pam."

Zoe didn't even have to look up into Desi's face to see the disgust in his eyes because she could literally feel it burning through her. She placed the phone back in her purse and mumbled, "I guess I better get out of here."

"Zoe, this has got to stop. It's time that you start living for you, sweetheart. I'll go pull the car around and when that waitress comes back with the check and my credit card, just sign my name, but don't over tip like you usually do."

The waitress returned with the bill and Zoe did as she was told and forged Desi's name, but despite his order, she tipped a generous twenty-five percent. That was ten percent more than Desi would have approved of. She grabbed her purse and headed out of the door, but just before she could exit the young man that was watching her earlier stepped in her path.

"Excuse me, ma'am, I don't mean to be disrespectful, but I couldn't help but see you crying earlier. You are far too beautiful to be crying like that, nothing or no one should ever make you that unhappy."

"Thank you for the kind words," Zoe blushed.

"Well I won't hold you; I know your man is probably waiting for you."

"Oh, Desi isn't my man, he's my best friend and yes, he is waiting. But thanks again and have a nice night." Zoe stepped around the guy, but he jumped back in her path.

"I promise I'll get out of your way, but I wanted to give you my card. I hope that you'll give me a call, maybe we could have dinner or something sometime."

Zoe graciously accepted his card and tucked it into her purse as she smiled and made her exit. She made a mental note to throw the card away as soon as she was out of the guy's line of vision. She'd heard everything that Desi said and would eventually start living for herself, but now was not the time.

CHAPTER SIX

As soon as Zoe crossed the threshold to her home she was pounced on. Pam literally ran and threw her arms around Zoe's neck as if she were a five year old greeting her parent.

"Pam, is all of this really necessary?" Zoe grunted as she reluctantly returned her sister's hug.

"You were gone so long, I was afraid something had happened to you. For a moment I even thought that maybe Otis had discovered where you worked or something," Pam exclaimed in her usual over exaggerated manner. "I was ready to call the cops."

"Did Mom not tell you that I called and said that I would be late? Didn't she tell you that I was going out to dinner with Desi?"

"Well yes, but I just didn't expect for you to be gone this long."

"Pam please! For the love of God, give your sister some breathing room. I'm sorry, Zoe, I told her to calm down and that you needed a little time for yourself. Did you enjoy your dinner, baby?" Martha quizzed.

"Yes ma'am, I enjoyed myself much more than I thought I would. It's been a long time since I've hung out like that. Desi and I had a great meal and even better conversation. Made me realize that I need more of that in my life."

"I agree, Zoe, you're a young woman and you should be living as such. We are safe and sound in a new city, miles away from Otis. It's time for you to start enjoying yourself more and worrying about us less, isn't that right Pam?"

"Yes ma'am," Pam sniffed. She knew that it wasn't fair for Zoe to be responsible for the three of them. She knew that her baby sister deserved to be free to go out and date and do all the things that young, beautiful women did, but she had hoped she'd have a little more time to adjust to the idea. Pam's sense of security was wrapped up in Zoe. She knew it wasn't fair, but she wasn't quite ready for it to change.

"Seriously guys, this was one simple evening out. Yes I'd like to have more evenings like tonight, but it's not like I'm going to be hanging out all the time. Pam, you can stop crying, I'm home and nothing has changed," Zoe explained with apparent agitation. "I'm tired and going to bed. Goodnight y'all."

Zoe escaped to her room, dropped her purse on the bed, and began to undress. The long hot shower that followed melted away the stress that had welcomed her home. As she dressed for bed, she replayed the conversation that she and Desi had shared and she knew that he was right when he said that it was time she started living for herself. She reached for her purse and the business card from the guy at the restaurant fell out.

"Ramon Martinez, Owner, ATL Building, Repair, and Remodeling," Zoe read aloud. She twirled the business card in her fingers as she remembered how handsome and kind he was. Then she tossed the card on her dresser, dismissing any thoughts of ever calling the guy. She clicked off her lamp, rolled over and fell asleep.

* * *

It had been three weeks since Zoe's outing with Desi and she was ready once again to have an evening out. As she finished dressing for work, Zoe went to her dresser to spray on a fine mist of perfume, but instead she found herself fondling the business card that the guy had given her the last time she was out with her best friend. She wasn't sure why she hadn't been able to throw it away, maybe it was just the thought that someone was interested in her that made her hold on to it. Finally she dropped the card, sprayed her perfume, and headed out the door for work. Whisking her car through the city streets, Zoe decided to call Desi and see if he had plans for the evening.

"Hey, how are you this morning?" Zoe almost sang into the phone.

"Hi, darling, as usual I'm running late for work, but I'm fine. What's up with you?'

"I thought I'd see if my bestie wanted to have dinner with me this evening? My treat…" Zoe added for good measure.

"Hey now, if it's free it's for me. What restaurant did you have in mind?"

"I thought we could go back to the place we went to a few weeks ago. I really liked the atmosphere and the food was pretty good as well."

"You sure you don't want to try someplace else? There are a million places to dine and a lot of them are better than where we ate."

"I'm sure there are and I promise, we will explore each and every one of them, but for tonight can we please go back?"

"I suppose so. Lord knows I can't turn down any opportunity to get you out in a social environment. Do you want me to pick you up at the credit union?"

"Are you sure you don't mind? I can try and find it on my own."

"Zoe please, everybody knows that you are directionally challenged. I'll be in the parking lot at 5:00."

"Thanks, love, I'll see you then."

Zoe assisted customer after customer with a smile on her

face and joy in her voice. Everyone that encountered her walked away feeling better than they did when they'd arrived. She had tried without success to put the idea of socializing with friends and even the possibility of dating out of her mind, but the thoughts kept invading her head. Three weeks of fantasizing about what could be had been enough for her. It was now time to live in the moment, time for her to start truly enjoying her life and just the prospect of it made her giggly.

April walked up to Zoe and smiled broadly. "Girl, I have never seen you so happy. I don't know what's going on, but I sure hope it continues."

April was the one and only coworker that Zoe allowed herself to get close to. All of the credit union's employees had welcomed her to their branch with open arms, but Zoe kept everyone at arm's length. But there was something about April that was very warm and comforting. She offered Zoe friendship without trying to pry into her personal life. She freely shared aspects of her life with Zoe, but never asked for information in return. And though April never asked, Zoe often found herself volunteering little tidbits of her life, her feelings, and opinions to her new friend. Zoe had never really had a close female friend and she was enjoying the growing closeness that she shared with April.

"Girl, I'm just happy to be getting out for a little R & R this evening. I'm going out with my friend Desi again for drinks. Would you like to tag along?"

"Oh…thanks, but I think I'll pass. I don't want to intrude on your night out."

"How is it an intrusion if I invited you?" Zoe asked sarcastically.

"Well if you don't think your friend would mind, I'd love to go. It's been a while since I've enjoyed a night out."

"Well he'll pick us up at 5:00pm and I guarantee we'll have a blast."

Fortunately, Desi was right on time. He watched as the

ladies approached his car, wondered who the beautiful woman was with Zoe, and humorously thought that if any woman could make him venture to the straight side of the road, it'd be her. The woman was just that attractive. Desi jumped out of the car for an introduction and to open the passenger door for Zoe.

"Hey, baby, how are you doing?" Zoe inquired as she threw her arms around Desi for a big hug, a peck on the cheek and she backed away. "Desi, this is my friend April. April this is my Desi." The two shook hands and exchanged pleasantries. "I hope you don't mind, but I invited April to hang out with us this evening."

"Of course I don't mind, any friend of yours is a friend of mine," Desi's smile confirmed his approval. Let me get the door for you lovely ladies and we'll be on our way. He opened the front, then the back passenger side doors and made sure each woman was in safely before closing the doors behind them. He dashed back around to the driver's seat and they were off for an evening of good food, great conversation and lots of laughter.

By the time the appetizers arrived with the second round of drinks, it seemed as if the three of them had been friends forever, like April belonged with them. The music was good and the energetic crowd only added to their already joyful mood. Periodically, Zoe would glance around as if she were looking for someone, but would quickly turn her attention back to her table.

"So, April, where are you originally from?" Desi asked the first of a long line of questions.

"I'm actually from Atlanta. Born and raised in the SWATS," April grinned with pride.

"What in the hell is the SWATS?" Zoe quizzed.

"Humph, that's what these homegrown country folks call southwest Atlanta. And all of them say it with such pride," Desi snorted sarcastically.

"You know, it kills me how all of you so called northerners come down here and complain about our traffic, call us country, can't understand the pride we have in our state, and so on. But what I don't understand is why y'all continue to stay. With all the complaining, I'd think you'd be trampling over each other to get back to wherever all you all came from," April ranted.

Zoe burst out laughing, "I guess she got you told."

"I guess she did," Desi admitted. "And now that I've been put in my place, I guess I'll keep the other questions I had to myself."

"Oh come on, don't be so sensitive. Now ask away, what else do you want to know?"

"Do you have a big family or are you one of those kids that have been spoiled rotten because you're an only child?"

"I used to have a twin brother, but sadly he died in a motorcycle accident a few years ago," April stated very somberly.

Zoe spoke in almost a whisper, "Oh, I had no idea, April; I can't imagine how hard that must have been for you."

"It was definitely the most difficult time in my life and it's something that I continue to struggle with," April admitted. "But, hey, everyone struggles with something, right?"

"Indeed they do," Desi confirmed. "I know I have my fair share of trials and tribulations."

April noticed that Zoe had gotten quiet and withdrawn. She was looking off into nothingness, her mind clearly flying over the territory where her own issues lie. "Zoe, are you okay? Zoe…"

Finally snapping out of her trance, Zoe offered a fake smile. "I'm all good, just listening to you guys."

"Well this is not what we came here for. This is supposed to be a happy time, so I propose we all take a shot and liven this thing up again."

April summoned the waitress, ordered three shots of Vodka and the laughter returned to their table. What didn't return to the table was Zoe's full attention. Both Desi and April noticed that she was constantly looking around, almost like she was casing the joint. With curiosity taking hold, April couldn't stop herself from asking Zoe what she was looking for.

Zoe blushed and hesitated before finally admitting that she thought maybe the guy she'd previously met there might have returned. Knowing they would ask a million questions, she immediately went on to tell them of the brief conversation she and the gentleman had shared and how he'd given her his phone number. "He seemed so nice and truly interested in me. That never happens…"

"What the hell are you talking about?" April looked puzzled by Zoe's untruth. "I have watched men drool over you on the daily. They come in the bank with dinner invitations and propositions for you all the time. We can't even go out to lunch without some dude hitting on you."

Desi studied Zoe's face, her perfect bone structure, almond shaped eyes, and flawless café mocha complexion. Her beautifully short, cropped hair and forever sexy red lips. How could she not see the attention that she commanded every time she stepped foot into any room? He thought of the brutality that she witnessed and suffered as a child and wondered if the effects of it still made her feel small or unworthy of the attention she commanded.

"April, you know just like I do that the clowns coming in and out of the bank are only joking around. They flirt with everyone and half of them are married." Zoe took a sip of her drink and looked around once more.

"What about the businessman with the expensive suits that comes in from time-to-time? He is gorgeous, smart, successful, single, and has asked you out no less than three times. You laugh him off as if he's cracking jokes or something."

Not having a good rebuttal, Zoe shrugged her shoulders and took another bite of her food. She could feel both her friends staring at her, neither fully understanding why she doubted how appealing she was to men or why she felt that the man from a few weeks ago was the only one she'd received any real attention from. Zoe knew that April had no idea about her childhood, but

Desmond knew it all and it confused her that he didn't understand her right now.

"Guys, we came here for some fun not a therapy session. I propose that we eat and drink up and then get out of here. After all, tomorrow is a work day."

Just as Zoe had requested, the three of them finished their meal, chatted about much of nothing, and headed back to the bank parking lot. April thanked them for a pleasant night out, jumped in her car, and headed home.

Desi held Zoe's hand until April was out of sight. He leaned against her car, looked in her eyes, and smiled. "If that guy from the restaurant is the only one that you think has come on to you or shown you any interest then it must be something special about him. Hundreds of knuckle heads see you, are interested in you, but if he's the only one that you've seen then you owe it to yourself to give him a call. Don't deprive yourself of companionship and please, please stop underestimating yourself. You're gorgeous, smart, and savvy, make him work for your affection."

Zoe smiled at her best friend, kissed him on the cheek, and climbed into her car. "You know me; I don't just give anything away. If I ever do decide to call him, he'll have to earn every minute of my time and affection."

"That's my girl," Desi smiled sweetly. "I love you."

"I love you too." Zoe closed her car door and took off. She mulled over everything that April and Desi had said. She wondered why she always blew off the advances from men, but couldn't seem to get the one guy out of her head. What was it about him that made her want to know more about who he was and what he was about?

After a hot shower, Zoe's bed was a welcome sight. It had been a long day and the drinks she had with dinner left her a little more mellow than usual. There was no doubt in her mind that a good, restful night's sleep was what she'd have. Zoe drifted off with thoughts of love dancing in her head. Sadly, it wasn't long before the face of love was replaced with that of Otis.

"It's your turn, baby girl."

His breath heavy with the scent of liquor and the sound of him slamming and locking the door caused Zoe to moan achingly. The image of him hovering over her removing his clothes made her squirm. The vision of her hitting him with the bank and beating him with the shard of porcelain sent tears streaming down her face. The heaviness of his body as he fell on top of her and the river of blood that flowed freely from his head sent screams of horror throughout the house.

"Zoe, wake up, baby, wake up. He's not here, honey, he's not here," Martha spoke soothingly as she wrapped her arms around her baby girl. She held Zoe until her screams and moans subsided.

CHAPTER SEVEN

Pam sat at the table with her sister and mother enjoying a delicious plate of homemade lasagna. She was especially happy, couldn't seem to wipe the smile off of her face. Zoe and Martha looked at her suspiciously; a genuine smile on Pam's face was as rare as a ten karat canary diamond.

"I can't take it anymore, Pam, please tell us what has you grinning like a chess cat?" Zoe quizzed. As she waited for the answer, she'd already imagined that it was something silly or trivial. At times it seemed that Otis' beatings had stunted Pam's maturity, leaving her an overgrown, silly, scared kid.

"I had lunch with one of our clients today. It was so nice that I accepted his invitation to dinner and a movie this weekend," Pam blushed.

Martha choked on her food and coughed uncontrollably. Pam jumped up and began to beat her mom on the back while simultaneously trying to pour water down her throat. Zoe offered no help, she was still too dumfounded by Pam's confession to move. Finally, after several minutes, Zoe regained her voice and Martha regained her composure. But still clearly shocked, Zoe asked, "So what brought this on? What made you even go to lunch with him? I mean you're twenty-eight and have only ever dated one guy and that only lasted a month."

"Thanks for the reminder, Zoe, but I'm very aware of my dating history, or lack thereof. But to answer your question, my supervisor had him come in for a lunch meeting, but then he got called away and asked me to meet with the client instead. His name is Alvin and he seems so nice, nothing like that controlling jerk I dated before."

"You can't get in trouble for dating him can you? Would it not be considered a conflict of interest?" Concern was written all over Martha's face.

"Not at all, during our meeting we discovered that my firm can't handle the type of accounts he has, they're too large for us. We've referred him to another accounting firm that would be a better fit for his business needs. And before y'all ask, yes, I'm sure I want to do this. I've talked at length with my therapist about getting out more and living a life that's normal and appropriate for someone my age. I trust her when she says that I can handle a relationship. This may or may not turn into a relationship, but if I don't at least go out with Alvin I'll never know."

Zoe didn't know what to say, she'd always felt like Pam was a child she had to protect, that's just how it had been. But now Pam was sounding so mature, talking more sensibly than they were used to. Zoe couldn't help but think that maybe seeing a therapist wouldn't be such a bad thing. If they could build this kind of confidence and growth in Pam, what could one do for her? As quickly as the thought came to her mind it was gone, she dismissed it feeling that she was of strong mind, will, and body and didn't need a therapist telling her how to move forward with her life.

"Wow, Pamela, I'm pleasantly surprised to hear you talking like this," Martha gushed as she began again to stuff her mouth with the Italian meal she'd prepared. As she chewed her food, she turned her head in Zoe's direction. The look on her face asked the question that her mouth was too full too verbalize.

"Mom, don't start. You can be happy for Pam without trying to throw me into the mix. I'm fine and we all know that I've started going out more and more with Desi and April. I enjoy every minute that I'm out with them and will continue to socialize and have a good time. So you can take that cute little question mark off of your cute little face," Zoe said with a smile.

"You want me to see if Alvin has a friend?" Pam snickered. They all burst into laughter knowing that Zoe would never allow anything like that.

Saturday rolled around and it felt as though they were getting Pam ready for her first prom. They had gone out and purchased her some new peep toe black pumps, a black blazer with a red blouse, and skinny jeans. She'd gotten her hair done earlier and Zoe treated her to a manicure and pedicure. Pam looked beautiful with her shoulder length, silky hair and rocking body. Stepping out of her normally old maid type clothing, she seemed to stand an extra two feet tall and had all the confidence in the world. The doorbell rang and the Shaw women giggled like school girls.

"Hi Alvin, come on in. Let me introduce you to my mom, Ms. Shaw and my sister, Zoe."

"Good evening ladies, it's a pleasure to meet you." Alvin nervously shook their hands.

"It's nice to meet you too, Alvin. So what are you guys doing tonight?" Zoe questioned.

"We have reservations at this nice little supper club downtown. I've heard the food is great and that the band is phenomenal." He turned his attention to Pam. "You do like music don't you?"

"Absolutely, sounds like we're in for a very entertaining night."

"Not too entertaining," Zoe warned as Martha elbowed her in the side in an attempt to shut her up.

"Well, on that note we're going to go before we miss our

reservation. Ladies, I'll see you both later." Pam turned and headed out the door on Alvin's arm.

"Looks like you're my date for the night," Martha joked.

"Get your shoes, old lady; let's go catch that new Tyler Perry movie."

"Really, Zoe?"

"Yeah, really. I might even splurge and buy you some overpriced popcorn."

CHAPTER EIGHT

What Zoe thought was impossible had actually happened. She had become inspired by her older sister. Over the past couple of months Pam's relationship with Alvin had blossomed. She was honest and forthcoming with him about her abusive past as well as her trust issues. He'd even accompanied her to a couple of her therapy sessions so that he could have a better understanding of her issues with intimacy. He was indeed Pam's Prince Charming, all because she opened her heart and allowed him to be.

Zoe sashayed over to the dresser and picked up the business card she'd received months ago. She'd tried to be more open to the men that showed interest in her, but none had captivated her the way that Ramon had. Finally she decided to stop fighting it and just call the man. After all, he might very well be her Prince Charming.

The phone rang twice as Zoe nervously bit her lip. Then that wonderfully masculine voice answered.

"This is Ramon, how may I help you?"

"Hi Ramon, my name is Zoe. You may not remember me, but we met briefly about three months ago. You stopped me as I was leaving -"

Ramon interrupted before she could finish trying to make

him remember her. "Of course I remember you. You had the gorgeous face with the sad eyes. I've been waiting for you to call."

"You have?" Zoe questioned.

"Yes indeed, what took you so long?" Ramon chuckled.

"I wasn't sure that I was ready to start dating."

"Did you just ask me out on a date?" Ramon teased. "I gladly accept, when should I pick you up?"

Zoe became flustered as she tried to correct her statement. "No I wasn't asking you out, I was just trying to explain that I didn't know if I was ready for the possibility of dating or if -"

"Zoe, it's ok, I was only teasing. There's no need to explain. But since the word was mentioned, will you please allow me to take you out on a date?"

"We know nothing about one another, Ramon. For all I know you could be a mad man," Zoe only half teased.

"Hmm... Let's see, I'm one of two children, I own my own business, I'm originally from Los Angeles, and my social security number is 222-88-8988. Now can we go out?"

With laughter in her voice, Zoe gladly accepted his offer. They talked for a few more minutes and after providing her address, Zoe disconnected the call. Smiling ear-to-ear, she was already looking forward to the time they would share Saturday evening.

For the first time in a long time, Zoe slept like a baby. Only pleasant dreams accompanied her throughout the night. She woke up refreshed and could hardly wait to get to work and share her news with April.

The day was flying by and Zoe had barely had a chance to even say hello to her friend. She was thankful that they'd both be able to get away for a late lunch. To save time, they decided to walk across the street to the deli. The food was okay, but the time they saved driving allotted them more time for conversation.

"So tell me, what has you looking all cheerful today?" April inquired as she took a bite of her turkey sandwich.

"I called him, girl, I finally called him," Zoe declared as she stirred a packet of sugar into her glass of iced tea.

"Okay, I have no idea who you're talking about. I mean can I get a clue, buy a vowel, or something?"

"You know, April, I forget what a sarcastic little thing you can be sometimes," Zoe giggled. "Remember I told you about the guy that stopped me as I was leaving the restaurant behind Desi? I finally worked up the nerve to call him." Zoe was all smiles as she shared her act of bravery.

"That's awesome, Zoe! So did he remember you, what did he say, is he interested in going out, and how many kids does he have?" April pelted Zoe with questions like hail does the ground during a storm.

"Damn, what ever happened to one question at a time?" Zoe asked rhetorically.

"Just answer me."

"Yes, his name is Ramon and he remembered me; he said that he'd been waiting for me to call. We're going out Saturday and I have no idea if he has kids or not. We didn't have a long, drawn out conversation which means we'll have plenty to discuss on our date."

April looked at Zoe with the sweetest smile on her face. "I'm happy for you, Zoe. More than any woman I know, you deserve a good man and true happiness. Who knows, Ramon just may be the man to give it to you."

"Let's hope so…," Zoe blushed.

"Oh gracious, I forgot to ask you the most important question of all. What are you going to wear?"

"That depends on what you help me pick out when we go shopping tomorrow." They giggled, finished their lunches and returned to work.

The week flew by. The shopping was done and Zoe was hoping that her nerves would fall into place just as her beautiful outfit had. For some reason she hadn't been able to shake this ongoing case of the jitters. Her excitement had turned to anxiety and she'd been threatening to call and cancel the date. But April, Pam, and her mom encouraged her to go and enjoy herself. They'd preached that she had to trust someone sometime and she'd be cheating herself if she didn't at least take this opportunity and give Ramon a chance. Desi on the other hand told her to go with her gut. He insisted that when Mr. Right came along she wouldn't have these kinds of doubts. However, knowing how overprotective Desi was, she didn't give much weight to his argument. In Desi's eyes no man would ever be good enough for her.

She was expecting the doorbell to ring any second, but until it did, she looked in the mirror and spoke positive affirmations. "This is just a date and it will go well. I am a beautiful woman inside and out and deserve to be in the company of a gentleman. God knows my heart and will protect it and me." Then it happened…ding dong. She took a deep breath and headed towards the living room only to see Desi coming through the door. "What are you doing here, Desi?"

"I came to meet this dude you're going out with and to see if I get any kind of bad vibe from him. You know if I do you're not going on this date."

"Desi, you do realize that I'm a grown woman and that this date is going to happen regardless of your vibe."

"I know you're grown, but -"

Zoe cut him off in mid-sentence, "It really wasn't a question, sweetheart."

The doorbell rang and Pam rushed to answer. She didn't want to keep Zoe's date waiting, but mostly she wanted to see what the guy looked like. She swung the door open and greeted him with a huge smile. "Hello, please come in. I'm Pamela, Zoe's sister," she almost sang as she extended her hand to shake his. Ramon shook her hand, offered a warm smile, and quickly scanned the room. "Hello everyone."

Zoe stepped forward with a smile on her face. He looked even better than he did when they first met. She drank in every detail, from his thick, dark, wavy hair to his bronze complexion and fine, well-toned 5 foot 11 inch body. "Hello, Ramon, it's nice to see you again."

"Zoe, you look beautiful." Clearly, everything about her physical appearance was pleasing to Ramon. The two of them stood in awe of one another until Desi reminded them that they were not alone when he rather loudly cleared his throat.

"Oh my goodness, where are my manners. Ramon, this is my mother, Ms. Shaw; my best friend in the entire world, Desi; and you've met my sister, Pam. Everyone, this is Ramon Martinez." Handshakes were given and pleasantries exchanged and after a little small talk, the couple was ready to leave for what would hopefully be a wonderful evening.

As they headed for the door Desi reached out for Zoe's hand and pulled her to him, whispering in her ear, "You don't have to go if you're not comfortable."

Zoe whispered back, "Do you see him, he's gorgeous. But don't worry, Dad, I won't be out too late," she teased and kissed him on the cheek before walking out the door.

The three that were left behind ran to the window to see Zoe ride off with Ramon in his beautiful, midnight black Infinity M37. "Wow, that's one good looking man. My baby sure knows how to pick 'em," Martha declared.

"You are right about that, Mama. That is a sexy little thing right there. I bet all of Zoe's apprehension flew out the window as soon as she laid eyes on him," Pam teased.

"Humph, I can't deny that he looks delicious," Desi chimed, "but it's just something about him that seems a little shady."

Martha gently placed her hands on Desi's cheeks and looked him in the eyes. "Anyone who dates Zoe is going to seem shady to you. You're over-protective and yes, I totally understand why, but you've got to let the girl go find her life. None of us want to see her alone and lonely for the rest of her days."

"You're right, but I swear if he does anything to hurt her I'll kill him."

CHAPTER NINE

Zoe sat quietly in the passenger seat as Ramon navigated the car through the city. He periodically glanced over at her, taking in her beauty. *Yeah, I can definitely work with this.* But he couldn't help but notice that she wasn't exactly comfortable in his presence.

"Are you okay over there?" he asked.

"Oh yes, I'm fine." Her response was curt and he wasn't sure if she even wanted to be out on this date.

"Zoe, you seem so uncomfortable and awfully quiet. Are you sure you're up for going out tonight?"

It was not her intent to come off so uptight. Zoe took a deep breath and gave Ramon a slight smile. "No, I absolutely want to go out tonight. I guess it's just been a while since I've dated and I've obviously forgotten how to relax and enjoy myself," she joked.

"I hear you, I haven't exactly been a dating machine myself," Ramon confessed.

"Yeah right, I find that a little hard to believe. I bet you're out with a different woman every week," she half joked.

Ramon grabbed his chest as if he were hurt. "Why would you say that? You know I'm a pretty shy guy, it takes a lot for me to even approach a woman," he spoke as if he were truly wounded.

"Well forgive me if I jumped to the wrong conclusion, but you didn't have any trouble approaching me."

"Actually, young lady, you approached me. It was you that left your table and headed my way, remember?"

Zoe couldn't help but laugh. The 'I'm so innocent' way he spoke and foolishness that he was saying were quite comical. "I didn't approach you, I was simply leaving the restaurant. If you remember correctly, I had to pass you in order to exit the building," Zoe chuckled.

"Woman please. You purposely let your friend go ahead of you and waited til I was positioned in your path before you even got up. Then you came walking up looking all good. I was hip to your little plan from the start."

The broad smile on Ramon's face was captivating and Zoe found herself all out laughing. He had used his charm and sense of humor to put her at ease and she liked that…a lot. Her body language and demeanor were now sending a different message, one of comfort and openness.

Ramon pulled into a downtown parking garage and the couple took the short walk through Centennial Olympic Park to one of Zoe's favorite steak houses. How could he have known how much she loved Ruth's Chris? They had the perfect table overlooking the park and the wine he suggested was divine. All nerves that either of them may have initially had had magically disappeared. While they waited for their meals to arrive, the conversation flowed like waterfalls.

"I want to know all about your life, Ramon. Where are you from, do you have a big family, how did you land in Atlanta?"

"Do you always fire questions off in sets of threes?" he teased.

"What can I say, enquiring minds want to know. So, start talking."

Ramon took a deep breath as if he were contemplating how

open he would be with Zoe. "Let's see, I'm originally from Los Angeles, but left the West Coast with my adoptive family when I was twelve. I have one brother, but we were split up and I haven't seen him since moving to Georgia." He found himself revealing more than he wanted because he knew that his answers would only lead to another question, a question that he hated supplying the answer to.

"Wow, I couldn't imagine being taken away from my sister. Do you mind if I ask what happened to your parents?" Zoe timidly asked.

"They died," he said flatly.

"Oh, I'm sorry." The way he replied and the change in his demeanor let Zoe know that she needed to step back from any further questions. She assumed that with time, he'd let her know how they died and if he's ever tried to reconnect with his brother. But for now, a change of subject was in order. "So, how do you like Atlanta? I'm still in my adjustment period and haven't really done enough to gauge how I'm going to like the city long term."

"You'll love it," he chirped in a much better tone. "There's a ton of great restaurants, decent night life, and some great excursions you can take at a moment's notice."

"Okay, well I'm not much of a club girl, but the excursions sound interesting."

"Oh yes, there's sky diving, white water rafting, zip lining-"

Zoe held up her hand. "You can stop right there cause I'm not jumping out of anybody's plane or swinging through the trees like Tarzan. I'm not quite that adventurous."

Laughing at her instant refusal of anything adventurous, he decided to suggest something a little tamer. "Then how about we keep it simple but fun with indoor rock climbing? That can be our next date," Ramon offered confidently.

Cocking her head to the side with a smile, Zoe asked "What makes you think they'll be a second date?"

"Just hoping," he responded with a wink.

Their dinner arrived and they enjoyed a great meal and interesting conversation. While they didn't revisit the topic of his parents, he did share with her how he came to be a business owner, the close relationship he has with his adoptive mother, and his hopes for the future. In turn, Zoe spoke about the unbreakable bond she had with her mother, sister, and Desi. She talked about her job and interests, but completely skipped over the topic of her father and the abuse she grew up with. He had not earned the right to know any of that yet.

Leaving the restaurant, he reached and held her hand as they strolled through the park. They stopped at the massive Ferris wheel that had recently been constructed and decided to take a ride. The view was amazing and Ramon pointed out all of the Atlanta landmarks. Before the ride ended, he leaned in and planted a gentle kiss on Zoe's cheek. It was beautiful and respectful, and Zoe was so glad that she hadn't allowed her nerves to cause her to miss out on this wonderful evening.

Ramon returned Zoe to her home and was already excited about their next date. As soon as Zoe crossed the threshold, her mom and sister hit her with a barrage of questions. But to their disappointment, Zoe hugged each of them and went off to bed with a smile on her face.

* * *

A few weeks had passed since Zoe's date with Ramon and every significant person in her life knew exactly how thrilled she was to have been in his company. As a matter of fact, she had been in his company four times since their initial date. The movies, dinners, and music concert had all been wonderful. Ramon had remained a gentleman and treated her like she was his queen bee. She now had no doubt as to whether she should open herself up to the possibility of falling in love.

But tonight there would be no Ramon; instead Zoe was going out to dinner with her number one guy, Desi. Over the past couple of weeks they'd talked on the phone as usual, but she missed seeing his handsome face. So in anticipation of their evening out, Zoe rushed through the Friday traffic, changed into something a little more suitable for a night out, kissed her mom goodnight, and dashed off to Desi's place.

Zoe parked the car and started walking across the parking lot towards the apartment building. She was caught off guard by the harsh sounds of fighting that echoed through the air. She hated arguments and cringed at the thought of a physical altercation. But the closer she got to Desi's door, the more she began to panic.

"Damn it, that's Desi and Kirk!" She tried to open the door and when she found it locked, began to bang on it like a mad woman. "Come on guys, open the door!" she shouted.

The sound of breaking glass sent a chill through her and she screamed threats of calling the cops if they didn't open the door. Finally, the lock clicked and the door cracked open. Zoe stepped in and was horrified to see both Desi and Kirk looking a battered mess and the living room trashed.

"What the hell are you two doing?" She demanded as she slammed the door closed. "Are y'all trying to go to jail tonight, 'cause if you think I'm the only one that heard you fighting then you're crazy." Zoe was so angry she could hardly get her words out.

"Your boy here got dudes calling my damn house like it ain't no big deal. Throwing these other knuckleheads up in my face like I'm some kind of punk," Kirk spat angrily.

"How many times and ways do I have to tell you that I'm not screwing around on you? Damn, it would be different if I was hiding the fact that I was talking to the guy. But like I've said a million times, its business." Desi stomped off to the kitchen to retrieve a paper towel to wipe his mouth.

"You have got to be kidding me, right? You two are in here fighting each other like two hoods on the street over a phone call! Don't you realize that if someone had called the cops you'd both be carted off to jail? And God knows that the last thing either of you need is a domestic violence charge." Zoe felt like a parent scolding her two boys.

"That's right, Zoe, take his side, I wouldn't expect you to do anything else," Kirk barked in her direction.

"I'm not taking anyone's side; I'm trying to keep both of you out of jail."

"Girl, save your breath, him and all his insecurities can't be reasoned with," Desi retorted.

"That's the funny thing, Desmond; I was never insecure until I started dealing with you. You flaunt your ass around like some damn queen, always gotta be the center of attention. Don't know how to talk to nobody without flirting. I can't deal with this shit no more. I'm tired of worrying who you're with and what you're doing."

"Fine, then I'm out cause I'm tired of it too." Desi stomped off to their bedroom, grabbed an overnight bag and began to throw his toiletries and a few clothing items inside. In a couple of minutes, he returned with two packed bags. "I'll be back tomorrow to get the rest of my shit."

"Desi wait, I'm sure Kirk didn't mean that he wanted you to leave. Did you, Kirk?"

"I've never asked him to leave, but it's what he always tries to do. This time I'm not stopping him."

"Come on, Zoe, let's go." Desi hung his head and walked out the door.

"I can't believe y'all are letting things end like this. There's been too much between you to walk away from each other so bitterly." Zoe wiped the tears from her face and followed Desi out the door.

Instead of an evening out, Zoe instructed Desi to head on over to her house and after picking up some take out and a couple of Redbox movies, she'd be right home. By the time Zoe walked in the house, Martha was comforting Desi with a plate full of her home cooking and sound motherly advice. Zoe tossed the pizza aside and joined them at the table. It wasn't long before the mood lightened and the three were laughing about old times back in DC. By midnight the laughter had dried up and they were all yawning. Desi thanked Martha with a big hug and kiss and then followed Zoe off to bed.

CHAPTER TEN

Pam crept through the front door at 8:00am. She walked ever so gently, trying her best to not alert anyone of her presence. She quietly padded into the kitchen and almost screamed when she saw Desi sitting at the table. "Boy, what are you doing here, trying to give me a heart attack?"

Desi chuckled softly, "What are you doing creeping in this time of day? You must have had one hell of a night."

"I had an okay night, nothing special and it's really none of your business," Pam replied with embarrassment. "You never answered my question, what are you doing here?" She demanded, trying to take the focus off of herself.

"Had a bad fight with Kirk last night and we decided to call it quits. I came back here with Zoe for the night."

"Oh, Desi, I'm so sorry," Pam sympathized as she made her way to the table and took a seat beside him. She took his hands in hers and looked him in the eyes. "Are you sure it's over? You know we tend to say so much in anger that we really don't mean. Maybe once you guys have had a chance to cool off and reevaluate the situation, you'll find that breaking up really isn't what either of you want."

"I hear what you're saying, Pam, but short of becoming a

monk there seems to be nothing I can do to convince Kirk that I'm faithful to him and to be honest, I'm tired of trying."

"But y'all love each other so much."

"Wasn't it Tina that said what's love got to do with it?"

"It has everything to do with it," she said as she gently released his hands. "How about some coffee?"

"OMG, Starbucks sounds so good right now."

"Child, nobody ain't said nothing about Starbucks. We got a coffee maker right here and three different flavors of cream." It didn't take but a hot minute for Pam to come up with two delicious cups of fresh brewed coffee.

"Okay, I'll give it to you, Pam, this is good coffee. Thank you. Now tell me, how was last night?" Desi asked with a devilish grin on his face.

Pam felt herself blushing like some little school girl. She ran her fingers over the round glass top table as if she were drawing the most pleasurable part of her night for all to see. "Desi, I had the best time. We went to a comedy show and out to dinner. I have never laughed so hard in my life. We really had a good time, but then we got back to Alvin's house and had an unbelievable time. Never have I experienced intimacy like that."

"Last night was you guys first time doing the horizontal Mamba?" Desi asked in disbelief.

"No, but it was the first time anyone ever did the oral thing to me. Desi, I thought I would crawl out of my skin. Whoa, I can't even talk about it, it was just that good."

"What was just that good?" Martha asked as she waddled through the doorway.

"Oh, good morning, Mama, I didn't know you were up," Pam stammered.

"That's because I just got up, but from the looks of things you never went to bed. At least not here. Now, what was just that good?" Martha continued to ask as she looked from Desi to Pam and back again.

"I was talking about the restaurant that Alvin took me to last night." Pam could hear Desi chuckle in the background and rolled her eyes in his direction. "It was an Asian bistro and the food was unbelievably good. I'll have to take you sometime, Mama; I think you'd really enjoy it."

"I'm sure I will. Now tell me, are you just getting home? And if so, don't you think you and Alvin may be moving a little too fast?"

"You're kidding right?" Zoe interjected as she entered the room. "Hell I was wondering what they were waiting for. They've been dating for what, like six, seven months now. I say it's about time and was it good?"

"Hells yes!" Pam exclaimed as she slapped her sister a high five. The four of them shared a hearty laugh and all Martha could do was shake her head. Yes, her daughters talked openly about everything in front of her and to her and she wouldn't have it any other way. She had been the best mother she was capable of being at the time, but clearly she had become a better friend to them than she had been a mom.

The laughter and conversation flowed as Martha began to move about the small kitchen in an effort to prepare breakfast. No one said anything about being hungry, but they were gathered and enjoying themselves. That's all the reason she needed to provide a small feast.

"Mama, don't cook too much because I won't be eating," Zoe advised.

"And why aren't you eating? You know that breakfast is the most important meal of the day." Martha cocked her head to the side waiting for an adequate reply.

"Oh, I'm going to have breakfast, just not here. Ramon is on his way to pick me up for brunch and then we're going on that rock climbing date I've been trying to avoid."

"Well excuse us, missy," Desi chimed. "I see you're letting Ramon pull out your adventurous side. If I had asked you to go rock climbing you'd have said no."

"Humph, well you never asked so we'll never really know

what my answer would have been. Besides, we all know that physical exertion is not something you consider fun."

"Maybe not *that* type of exertion, but give me the right dude and-"

"Okay, okay, that's enough of that conversation," Martha interrupted. "It sounds like you and Ramon have a fun filled day planned, baby. Just be careful, I don't want you coming back here with any broken bones."

"No worries, Mama, they have safety measures in place to protect against all that," Zoe assured.

It wasn't long before Martha was placing platters of biscuits with gravy, sausage, scrambled eggs with cheese, and home fries in the center of the table. Everything looked and smelled so delectable that even Zoe was about to fill a plate with food when the doorbell rang. She sighed deeply, put the empty plate down and headed for the door.

"Good morning," she chirped gleefully as she swung the door open.

"Hello, gorgeous, how are you today?" Ramon smiled sweetly as he greeted Zoe with a warm embrace.

"I am doing great. Come on in, everyone's in the kitchen having breakfast. We can either eat here or go to Mimi's Café as planned." Zoe led the way to the kitchen and Ramon followed closely behind, admiring every physical feature about Zoe.

"Good morning everyone," Ramon greeted as he entered the kitchen. He was about to speak again but was caught off guard by the presence of Desi.

"Good morning," everyone seemed to have chimed the salutation in unison.

Placing mugs of coffee on the table, Martha offered, "Why don't you guys have a seat and join us for breakfast?"

"Thank you, it all looks delicious, but I promised this young lady some of Mimi's famous French toast," Ramon countered as he placed his hand in the small of Zoe's back. "But next time we promise to join y'all. Who knows, I may even cook breakfast for you, Ms. Martha," he teased.

"Gotta love a man in the kitchen," Desi interjected.

"I know," offered Pam. "I love it when Alvin cooks for me."

"Yeah, he loves your meals too," Desi said sarcastically.

"Alright, I see you guys are about to start tripping. Talking mess that my virgin ears don't want to hear. Come on, Ramon, let's get out of here." Zoe took Ramon by the hand and led him back out of the apartment as he shouted goodbye to everyone.

As Ramon headed up Highway 85 North he couldn't help but ask the question that he'd wanted to ask since he first stepped into the kitchen and greeted everyone. "Babe, what was Desi doing at your place so early?"

"Oh, poor thing, he and Kirk had a bad fight last night and he ended up spending the night with us. Those two love each other so much, but Kirk's jealousy is driving a serious wedge between them. I don't know if they'll be able to work it out this time."

"So where did he sleep? It's not like y'all have an extra bedroom."

"He slept with me," Zoe said very nonchalantly.

Ramon cut his eyes in her direction with a very unpleasant look on his face. He was clearly not pleased by her revelation. "Do you think it's appropriate to be sharing your bed with a male that's not your significant other?"

"Oh please... Desi is not just my best friend, he's like my brother. Besides you know he's gay, it's not like there's a possibility for any hanky panky. Physically I don't have a thing that Desi wants," Zoe chuckled as she took note of the fact that Ramon was still less than amused. She couldn't understand why he seemed so annoyed with the fact that she and Desi had shared a bed. Obviously it was all innocent, hell they had been sleeping together since they were kids and she'd escape over to his house to seek refuge from Otis.

Ramon pulled the car over onto a side street and threw it in park. "Babe, I would never try to discourage your friendship with Desi or anyone else, but I will ask you to please consider not sleeping with him again. It doesn't look good, sound good, and I'm just not comfortable with it. I know that he's been there for you for years and I'm new on the scene, but I'm crazy about you. I want us to build something strong and lasting. I respect you guys' friendship and welcome him as a friend of mine, but please promise me that you won't share a bed with him or any other man as long as we're involved?"

Zoe was immediately put off by his request. In her mind, this was his attempt to control some aspect of her life. If she gave into this request, what would he ask for next? "I'm sorry, but I can't promise that. Desi has been there for me in ways you can never imagine. So if it's a place to sleep he needs, I'm more than happy to provide that. Even if it means sleeping with me," she responded very matter-of-factly.

Ramon looked wounded by her immediate refusal. "Wow, such a simple request and you wouldn't even consider it. What does that say about us and the relationship we're trying to build?"

Stone faced, Zoe simply answered, "It means that you need to learn to trust me."

CHAPTER ELEVEN

It had been a crazy day and the customers were driving Zoe insane. Everything and everyone seemed to be tap dancing on her nerves. She'd even found herself snapping at April, something she'd immediately regretted. Her apology was an offer to buy lunch and thankfully, April accepted.

"So tell me, Zoe, what has you so upset today? You're not acting at all like your normal self. I've never seen you so on edge," April declared as she took a big bite of her cheese-burger.

"Let's just say that I had a moment with Ramon this weekend and it left a really bad taste in my mouth. I swear I've been annoyed ever since Saturday."

"Okay, so what was the moment? I mean how bad could it have been?"

"Long story short, Desi and his partner had a bad fight Friday and Desi went home with me. He spent the night with me, slept in the bed with me and Ramon apparently had a huge problem with it. Had the nerve to try and make me promise that Desi would never sleep with me again. Can you believe that?"

April chewed slowly as she looked around the restaurant clearly avoiding eye contact with Zoe. But after a few seconds she could feel her friend's eyes burning a hole in her, demanding a reply. "I'm sorry, Zoe, but that doesn't sound like such an unreasonable request to me. No man wants to think of his woman sharing a bed with another man."

"Oh come on, April, we all know that Desi is gay. He has no interest in anything a woman has to offer. Especially me, I'm like a sister to him for goodness sake!"

"Girl, I'm going to need for you to calm down and lower your voice," April instructed as she took note of the people in the small diner looking their way. "You asked me a question; you can't get salty because you don't like my answer. And I'm not the kind of friend that only tells you what you want to hear, I tell you how I truthfully feel. I understand that Desi is gay, but that doesn't change the fact that he's still a man and that is obviously threatening to Ramon."

"Clearly we view this differently. To me it seems as if he's trying to control me. This is how it all starts, they convince you to give up something or someone important to you. Once you cave on one thing, they demand something else until everything and everyone you've ever cared about is cut out of your life and all that remains is them." Zoe's voice was shaky and tears danced on the rim of her eyes, threatening to fall down her cheeks.

April reached across the table and took Zoe's hand in hers. "Honey, why are you so emotional about this and who are you referring to when you say 'they' and 'them'?"

"I'm referring to men, they are all the same, they all want to control every aspect of their mate's life and I can't have that. I won't allow any man to control my life," Zoe sobbed.

"Zoe, don't you think that you may be reading a little bit too much into his request? I mean I'll be the first to admit that some men are controlling, but not all of them. There are so many good men out there and I'd hate for you to throw away one of those good men because of one request he made. Which, by the way, he probably only made because he's feeling insecure in this new relationship."

"I don't know, April. My mother has spent her entire life

either being controlled or dealing with the fall out of being controlled. I won't be my mother; I refuse to live her life."

"And I would never want you to live that life, but I do want you to be sure of Ramon's intensions before throwing him away. Talk to him, Zoe, and be clear with him just like you were with me. Give him the opportunity to either confirm your fears or show you that he has no desire to control you at all."

Ramon had called Zoe multiple times since their date on Saturday, but Zoe had refused to answer his calls. He left voice mail messages apologizing for any misunderstanding and practically begged for her to return his call. But it was all in vain, Zoe simply deleted each message.

As she put the key in the apartment door, Zoe was replaying her earlier conversation with April. Maybe she was jumping the gun on ending her involvement with Ramon. Maybe she did need to let him clarify his position. Or maybe she had been right all along and his intent was to start controlling every aspect of her life. She closed the door and hoped that she'd have the place to herself for a little bit, but that was too much to hope for. Desi had apparently been hanging out there all day.

"Hi there, baby doll. How are you doing today?" Desi asked in an upbeat voice.

Zoe plopped down on the sofa beside him. "It was okay I suppose."

"You don't look or sound like it was okay. You look like you're exhausted and sound annoyed as hell," Desi observed. "Lean on my shoulder and tell me what's the matter."

Zoe snuggled into the old, tan couch, leaned on Desi and contemplated whether or not she should tell Desi about her issue with Ramon. Finally after an awkward silence, Zoe thought 'what the hell' and blurted it all out. The entire story and not once did she try to clean up what Ramon had said. Once she was finished, knowing he would be furious, she braced herself for Desi's reply.

"Okay, what else did he say 'cause that's not enough to

warrant your reaction? I mean I'm not the biggest fan of the dude, but you've got to give me more."

"How much more do you want? Wouldn't you be outraged if Kirk tried to drive a wedge between us?" Zoe had such a look of confusion etched across her face.

"Girl please! You have to know that everyone is not going to understand our relationship. Do you have any idea how many times Kirk has accused me of being bisexual because of my relationship with you? Folks feel threatened by what they don't understand. Clearly Ramon and Kirk have never had a friendship with someone of the opposite sex that's as close as ours and that's okay. You just have to reassure him, make him know that he's the only one you're interested in romantically."

"I don't know, Desi, it seems to me like this is the first step in him trying to control my life, keep me under his thumb."

"No, no, sweetie, you can't do that. You can't suspect every man of being another Otis. It's not fair to the man in your life and it's not fair to you."

Zoe laid her head on his shoulder once again. "But what if he is the next Otis?"

"But what if he's not?" Desi asked.

* * *

The doorbell rang and Zoe wasted no time letting Ramon in. After her conversation with Desi, she called Ramon and invited him over so that they could clear the air. Overhearing her phone conversation, Desi decided to leave and give them an opportunity to have this little discussion in private.

"Come on in and have a seat," Zoe offered with a half-smile on her face.

Ramon leaned down and gave her a peck on the cheek as he passed her on his way to the couch. "I was glad to get your call. You had me worried that I'd never hear from you or see you again. It seemed that we were going to end before we really had a chance to begin," he confessed.

Zoe took a seat next to Ramon, placed her hand on his and began to speak. "I'm sorry for my harsh reaction. I guess there are some things that I need to explain. You see, I grew up in an abusive home. I watched my father beat my mother and my sister and as I got older, he turned his brutal attention to me. The things he did to us were unspeakable and it all started because my mother wasn't aware of the early signs of his possessive and abusive behavior. He disguised his need to control her as love and a desire to always have her close. So I took your request about me and Desi as a sign of control and possessiveness."

Ramon had listened intently to what Zoe was saying and he decided that a little confession of his own was in order. "Babe, when you asked about my parents, I told you that they died but I didn't say how. For years I watched my father abuse my mother and when his jealousy became too much for him to handle, he shot her dead right in front of me and then turned the gun on himself. If my father taught me one thing, it was how not to treat a woman. I would never try to control you, I would never hurt you. I've seen first-hand what that abusive mentality can do and I promise you, none of that will ever be a part of our relationship."

His confession and tears that threatened to fall broke Zoe's heart. She wrapped her arms around him and rested her head on his chest. He returned her embrace and was glad that they'd both felt safe enough to share their past.

CHAPTER TWELVE

Three months after Zoe and Ramon had their little heart-to-heart, things couldn't be better. They'd agreed to immediately talk through any disagreements and to be honest and forthcoming with their feelings instead of shutting one another out. Refusing to go to therapy herself, these were tid-bits that Zoe had taken from Pam's therapy and implemented in her and Ramon's relationship. She felt that this was the best advice Pam had been given and the only useful part of her therapy. Despite Pam's pleas for Zoe to also attend therapy, Zoe felt that she wasn't nearly as damaged as Pam and just didn't need it. Besides, things were great now and therapy wasn't necessary.

Martha had gone to the store and purchased a ton of food. Sunday always meant a good meal, but since they would be joined by Ramon, Alvin, Desi, and Kirk she decided to really go all out. They were all overjoyed that after a month apart, Desi and Kirk realized that they belonged together and were able to work things out.

"Mama, it smells wonderful in here. What all are we having and what can I do to help?" Pam quizzed as she entered the kitchen.

"I'm preparing Cornish hens, cornbread dressing, greens,

yams, a little okra, and strawberry shortcake. And I appreciate your offer to help, but we all know that you can't cook," Martha snickered.

"Oh, that's cold, Mama. I can cook a little bit."

"I know you can, baby, but I'm almost finished. What you can do is set the table for me."

Martha pointed out the table-cloth, napkins, and silverware that would adorn the long fold out table she'd set up in the living room to accommodate everyone. Pam was glad to do her part and set the table. She even took an empty basket and the flowers she'd received from Alvin and made a beautiful centerpiece.

Zoe walked in the door with a couple of bottles of wine and immediately took notice of the table. "Wow, Pam, that's beautiful," she complimented.

"Thank you. What kind of wine did you get?"

"For Cornish hen, the guy at the Niko's Wine Corner suggested a good Merlot so I went with that," Zoe said as she breezed on into the kitchen. "Hey, Mama, I'm back. It sure does smell good in here. Anything I can do to help?"

"Nope, I've got it all under control. But I think I forgot to tell your sister to put the wine and water glasses on the table," Martha said as she crooked her head to the side.

"Well she has them on there. That table is set beautifully." Zoe placed the wine bottles on the counter and leaned back contemplating how her mother would react to her next question. "Mama, do you ever think about how it would be to meet someone new? You know, a man?"

"Where in the world did that come from?" Martha looked at Zoe as if she had grown a second head.

"I'm just curious."

"Curious about what?" Pam inquired as she entered the kitchen.

"Your sister is in here talking craziness," Martha declared.

"Asking if I've thought about meeting men. I need a man like I need to be punched in the eye."

"Mama, all men are not abusive. There are still some really great, respectful, caring men out there. You shouldn't close yourself off to the possibility of meeting one of them," Pam spoke so assuredly. Martha and Zoe wasn't sure if it was Alvin, the therapy, or a combination of the two, but Pam was stronger than ever in every aspect of her life. They used to blow her off, but not anymore. Pam commanded respect and her words resonated with truth.

"I couldn't have said it better myself," Zoe smiled in agreement with Pam. "Mama, you see that the two of us were fortunate enough to land great guys and the same thing could happen for you."

Martha spun around in a bit of a huff. "Look, I know y'all mean well and I'm glad that you've both ended up in great relationships. But I have no interest in meeting anyone. I have had enough headaches and heartaches caused by men to last me three lifetimes. Thank you for thinking of me, but I'm not interested."

"Mama, I only asked because I met this wonderful, older gentleman in the store today. He's handsome, retired, and a widower. He was the first to suggest the wine I bought for-"

Martha slammed a pan against the counter and cut Zoe off mid-sentence. "Didn't I say that I was not interested? I know I didn't stutter. Now I appreciate and love y'all for wanting me to be with someone, but that is not something that I want for myself. I am happy and content right now and I plan to stay that way all by myself. This conversation is done. Now what time is everyone supposed to arrive?"

Pam hung her head and whimpered, "Alvin will be here in about twenty minutes."

"Everyone should be here in the next twenty to thirty minutes," Zoe added. "And, Mama I didn't mean to upset you, I meant no harm. I'm sorry."

"It's okay, baby, no apologies required. I know that y'all meant well and I love you for wanting me to be happy, but I promise you that I already am. This is the most content I've been in a long time. I'm totally at peace with my life."

"Then that's all that matters, Mama," Pam declared as she leaned in and kissed Martha on the cheek.

It wasn't long before the doorbell rang and their guests began to pour in. The Shaw women placed platters and bowls of food on the table. Martha, being the head of the house, led everyone in prayer and they began to dig in. The conversation flowed and the clinking of silverware on the plates signified how much everyone was enjoying the feast that had been set before them.

"Ms. Martha, this is the best meal I've ever had," Desi confessed as he continued to shovel fork fulls of greens and yams in his mouth. "And Lord knows I've had plenty of your cooking. This must have been made with an extra dash of love."

Martha blushed. "Desi, flattery will get you far, but it won't get you extra helpings of dessert," she chuckled.

Everyone burst out laughing. Desi hung his head and pretended to be wounded by Martha's words. "I didn't want extra helpings anyway."

Kirk laughed so hard that food almost flew out of his mouth. "Don't believe him, Ms. Martha, all he's been talking about is how delicious your desserts are. He'll be begging for seconds before he finishes the first helping."

Once again laughter filled the air. Desi playfully elbowed Kirk in the side. "Did I ever tell you that you talk too much? If not, I meant to."

Once Zoe and Pam cleared the table, Martha emerged from the kitchen with a tray of scrumptious strawberry shortcakes. Everyone oohed and ahhed at how good they looked, but once they tasted them, a look of pure joy seemed to cover everyone's face.

"Ms. Martha, I have never tasted whipped cream this good," Ramon remarked.

"That's because she makes it from scratch and with love. Mama has never used cream from a tub or can," Zoe bragged as if the compliment had been paid to her instead of her mother.

"Everything I've ever eaten over here has been exceptional, Ms. Martha. You are a gifted woman," Alvin complimented.

"Can you cook this well, Zoe?" Ramon asked excitedly.

"I...I...do okay," she stuttered.

"There was a lot of hesitation there, babe," Ramon replied. Then he heard the faint sounds of snickering coming from everyone else at the table. "Humph, she can't cook huh?"

"My baby girl does her best and no one can ask for more than that," Martha replied sweetly.

"Well maybe once she moves in with me we can get cooking lessons for us both so that we don't starve," Ramon blurted out. Instantly, there was a shift in the room, a change in the atmosphere.

"Zoe, are you planning to move in with him?" Pam asked as she squinted her eyes like the thought of it was causing her pain.

Everyone held their collective breath as they waited for her answer. Looking into the concerned faces of her loved ones, Zoe was almost too scared to answer. Usually strong and assertive, she averted her eyes, hung her head and finally spoke softly. "Ramon and I have been talking about it for a little while and yes, I've agreed to move in with him."

Martha got up from the table, placed her dessert plate in the kitchen sink, and went off to her room without uttering a sound. Her silence said more than any string of words ever could.

"Are you sure you're ready for this, Zoe? I mean this is still a relatively new relationship," Desi stated in a condemning voice.

"Look-"

"No, you look," Pam interrupted. "People know each other for years before making a move like this. No offense, Ramon, but how well do you really know him? Have you had time to learn all of his little idiosyncrasies? Have y'all even discussed how you'll conduct your household, split the bills?"

"Well damn, Pam, I thought we were cool," Ramon asserted in too loud of a voice. "You act like I'm going to run off with her and throw her in a cave or something. Hell, I ain't trying to steal her from you or nothing," he growled.

"Okay, let's take it down a notch or two y'all," Desi said in a calm voice. "Please understand, Ramon, Pam is just concerned for her sister."

"And let me guess, you're concerned too? After all, she is like your sister," Ramon stated sarcastically.

"Look dude, I'm just trying to keep things calm. Your attitude is not necessary." Desi's tone was no longer calm and soothing and Zoe knew that if this continued it would only get uglier.

"I want all of y'all to chill the hell out. My mama went through the trouble of preparing this fabulous meal for us and now the day is turning into some kind of circus. Pam, I never meant for you guys to find out like this. I'd planned to talk to you and Mama tonight," Zoe said as she cut her eyes at Ramon. "So now that everyone is done eating, I'm going to ask Ramon, Alvin, and Kirk to excuse us so that I can discuss this with my family. I need to check on my mama."

Alvin and Kirk got up from the table and gave their mates a hug and kiss as they prepared to leave. Ramon, on the other hand, remained in his seat. Zoe looked at him as to say 'get your ass up' but her stare wasn't enough to move him.

"If y'all are going to be talking about me I should at least be here to defend myself," Ramon remarked as he stared straight ahead.

"Baby, you have nothing to defend yourself against. I just want to talk to my family. I'll call you in a little while," Zoe said in a stern voice. Hesitantly, Ramon got up and headed out the door with the others.

Zoe eased back to her mother's room and gently knocked on

the door. "Mama, would you please come out here so that I can talk to you guys about this. Only family is here, everyone else has left. Please come out, Mama." She heard the lock click and her mother slowly opened the door. "Come on out, Mama, the four of us need to talk about this."

Martha walked back to the living room looking as if her puppy had just died. She sat down, took a deep breath and asked, "Why, Zoe? Why do you feel the need to move in with this man?"

"Mama, I love him."

"I love Alvin, but you don't see me packing my bags," Pam exclaimed as she sat nervously wringing her hands.

"Come on guys, hear me out. I feel that I have been taking care of everyone all my life and I've been glad to do whatever was necessary to care for us. But now I have someone that wants to care for me, he wants to protect me, love and support me, and the thought of that makes me happy. Don't y'all want me to be happy?"

Martha's eyes pond up with tears. "I didn't know we had been such a burden to you. All this time I thought that we were here for one another. I didn't realize that you felt that you were supporting us and getting nothing in return."

"That's not what I meant, Mama-"

"But that's what you said," Pam interrupted.

"You all are not being fair; you know I didn't mean it like that. I don't think I could have ever made it without y'all. We have supported one another. I'm just saying that I want to have the opportunity to build a life with a man that loves me. I want the chance to see if I can successfully live with him, possibly marry him, build a family with him. I just want to try," Zoe whimpered as she pleaded her case.

Desi knew that this was a big step for Zoe and not an easy one to take. He could only imagine how long she'd stressed over having to tell them about this decision, but he wanted to make sure that she hadn't been pressured into this move by Ramon.

"Zoe, no one wants to deny you your happiness or the chance to build a new life with your man. What we do want though is to be sure that this is what you want. My only concern is that you may be moving a little too soon on this. Did Ramon pressure you about moving in with him?" Desi asked.

"Seriously, Desi, I can't believe you're even asking me that. All of you should know by now that I don't do anything I don't want to and I've never succumbed to pressure. I'm stronger than that," Zoe exclaimed. "I know he may not be the man y'all may have imagined for me, but he's a good guy and again, he loves me."

"No one has anything against Ramon. He's a nice guy that clearly makes you happy, but"

"Humph, Alvin says it's something not quit right about him," Pam interrupted Martha in mid-sentence.

Martha threw Pam an ugly look. "Like I was saying," Martha continued, "we have nothing against Ramon and I hear you loud and clear when you say that he loves you, but I have yet to hear you profess your love for him. Are your feelings for him as strong as his are for you? And for the love of God, please don't make a decision to move in with this man just to prove that you're beyond all the hell that your father put us through. You haven't had the benefit of counseling and may need to do a little more self-discovery before jumping into a new living situation. I want you to be sure, baby, and more than anything I want to see my girls happy and not hurt."

"Look, I appreciate you all's concern, but contrary to what you believe, I do love Ramon. I don't need therapy to know what or who I want. Y'all are my family, I love you and will always make y'all a priority in my life, but my decision has been made. Next month I'll be moving in with Ramon and that's that!"

CHAPTER THIRTEEN

Unlike everyone else, April was excited for Zoe and her decision to move in with Ramon. After discovering that Ramon had a typical bachelors pad with very few of the essentials, she'd finally convinced Zoe to go shopping with her. April wanted to treat her friend to some of the necessities that would turn Ramon's house into their home.

It had been a long week and the credit union had been crazy busy. Everyone was a little burned out and at five o'clock, the manager locked the doors and all of the employees hurried to get out of the building and begin enjoying their weekend. April and Zoe were no exception. "We still on for drinks, right?" April asked as they exited the building.

"Girl, yes! I'll meet you at Taco Mac, and if you get there before me go ahead and order me a strawberry margarita," Zoe instructed.

"Will do and don't be long, Zoe. I know you're gonna call and check in with your man, but don't have me sitting there forever."

The restaurant was pretty full, but April was able to snag one of the last available booths. She ordered two margaritas, chips and salsa. Luckily, the Hawks vs. Grizzlies game was on. April knew that her hometown team didn't stand much of a chance against the Miami Heat, but surely they could beat the Memphis Grizzlies. Forty-five minutes later, April had drunk both margaritas, ate the chips and salsa, and watched her team lose. Her patience had run out and she was putting her jacket on to leave when Zoe finally approached the table. "I am so sorry for keeping you waiting so long," she apologized as she took a seat opposite April.

Annoyed, April tossed her jacket back in the seat and plopped herself down. "What the hell took you so long?"

"Can you believe that I was in the car talking to Ramon? Girl he was acting like his life was going to fall apart because I was hanging out with you for a while. You'd think I was his only friend in the world."

"Is he always this way? I mean will you still be able to hang out with your friends once you guys are living together?"

"Of course," Zoe reassured her. "We may be living together, but we'll still have time to do our own thing. Any healthy relationship allows for a little time away from each other."

"Just checking. I wouldn't want old boy to hold you captive away from the rest of the world," April said with a half-smile on her face.

"That's something you never have to worry about. I refuse to give my freedom up for anybody!"

The waitress retuned and they placed an order for another round of drinks and an appetizer platter. They laughed, joked, but also shared serious conversation. It wasn't long before Desi's name came up and they decided to call him and see if he could join them for a short while. Shortly after, he dashed through the door and joined the girls for a little gossip and a few laughs. The only annoying part of the evening was the constant buzzing of Zoe's cell phone.

"Damn girl, who is trying to reach you and what is their emergency?" Desi quizzed with a slightly annoyed look on his face.

"It's just Ramon. He wants to know what time I'm swinging by his place." Zoe had barely finished her sentence when the phone buzzed again.

"Damn, enough already," Desi shouted. He then took the phone from Zoe's hand, turned it off and kept it on his side of the table. Without the unyielding buzzing, the three of them were able to enjoy the rest of their evening in peace.

A couple of hours later the threesome said their goodbye's and went their separate ways. Before pulling off, Zoe decided to turn her phone back on and was shocked to see more than ten messages from Ramon. Thinking something was wrong, she hastily called him back. "Hey, baby, is everything okay? Was there an accident or something?" Zoe asked anxiously.

"And if there had been, what would it have mattered to you," Ramon replied in a cold voice. "I could've been dead for all you know. Why didn't you return any of my messages, Zoe?"

"Ramon, you had already texted me so much that I couldn't get a word of conversation in with my friends because I was too busy communicating with you. It was rude to keep replying to you and ignoring them. Not to mention that the constant buzzing and dinging was annoying to the other patrons. I was trying to be considerate." Zoe found herself becoming annoyed with his needy, clingy behavior. This was a new element to their relationship and she didn't like it one bit.

"Fine, Zoe, take your considerate ass on home then. If I'm that much of a bother, just keep rolling right on past my place."

"Fine, I will!" Zoe threw the phone into the passenger seat and started her car.

Apparently Ramon didn't know her as well as he should, but she felt it was time he learn a few things. One thing she despised was for someone to try and guilt trip her. It was simply unacceptable.

She was about to turn into her complex when her cell phone rang. "Yes?"

"So that's how you answering the phone now?"

"Look, Ramon, I don't have the time nor the patience for these games."

"Calm down, Zoe, I was just calling to apologize. I had no business blowing your phone up like that. I should've respected your time with your friends. I'm really sorry, now please come over here. I've missed you today and want nothing more than to see you."

"I appreciate and accept your apology, but I've already made it home. I'm about to get out of the car now and get ready for bed."

"You can get ready for bed over here," Ramon said seductively. "And I promise to give it to you so good that you'll sleep like a new-born baby. Now bring your sexy ass over here."

Zoe blushed like a little school girl and before she knew it, she was backing her car up and heading to Ramon's with expectations of being screwed out of her mind.

* * *

Sex in the morning was always a good way to start the day. So when Zoe left Ramon's place, she was all smiles. She'd run home, changed her clothes, spent some time with Martha and Pam, and was now sitting in April's drive way. They were heading out for a day of shopping and Zoe couldn't deny that she was excited about it. She'd envisioned the types of things she wanted to get for the house, the curtains, towels, and dishes, everything that would transform Ramon's house into their home.

"Hey, girl, are you ready to go break the bank?" April laughed as she hopped in the passenger seat.

"I don't know about breaking any banks, but we will most definitely get our shopping on. Where do you think we should start, Bed Bath & Beyond?"

"How about we hit the mall first? Macy's is having a home sale and we get an additional twenty-five percent off when we use the Macy's card."

"April, you sound like a damn commercial and I don't even have a Macy's card," Zoe stated with laughter in her voice.

"Well I have a card, plus I want to check out a couple of other stores. Is that cool with you?"

"Yes, girlie, that's cool."

Zoe maneuvered through the city streets and eventually made her way to Highway 85. They both loved the Mall of Georgia so there was no debate as to which mall would get their money.

April played with the radio nobs until she found a station that was playing some smooth R&B music. She had promised herself that she wouldn't be all nosey and ask Zoe anything about Ramon's behavior last night when she finally returned his calls. But she soon discovered that that wasn't a promise she was capable of keeping.

"So, how was Ramon last night? Was he pissed that you turned off your phone?"

"He wasn't pissed. He tried to act all hurt and give me some guilt trip, but I didn't hesitate to let him know that his behavior wasn't cool. It didn't take him long to call me back apologizing."

"Dang, girl, sounds like you laid down the law," April teased. "We know who the boss of that relationship is. You'll probably move in and have that poor man washing your drawers and cooking your meals."

"I don't know about all that, but I do know that we'll have a partnership. We'll share the housework and I'm more than happy to contribute equally to the household. But what I'm not willing to do is move in and be his maid or act like June Cleaver, following all her man's instructions and waiting on him hand a foot. That's for the birds."

"Yeah, you talk a good game, Zoe, but you'll probably be over there doing any and everything to keep your man happy. He'll say jump and you'll ask how high," April laughed hysterically at her little joke.

Zoe looked at her stone faced, "That will never happen. I'd die before I allowed myself to become that kind of woman."

"Gracious girl, I was only kidding. Lighten up a little. Where's that sense of humor?"

"Oh, I guess I did get pretty serious, huh?" Zoe asked as she offered up a bit of a smile. "My bad, sometimes I get a little carried away at the thought of being dominated by some knuckle head." As she continued down the highway a sign for Cracker Barrel caught Zoe's eye. "Have you eaten," she asked.

"I ate a piece of toast and had a cup of coffee. Why?"

"I could use a bite. How do you feel about a little breakfast?"

"Sounds good to me," April said cheerfully.

Luckily the place wasn't crowded and in a matter of minutes, they were served pancakes, hash browns, bacon, and coffee. And it was at this time that Zoe decided to share a little more about her past life with April. She wanted her friend to understand where she was coming from earlier and not just think she was crazy.

"April, we've had a lot of great talks and I appreciate you so much, but there is a lot I haven't shared with you."

"Yes, I'm aware. I know very little about your pre-Atlanta life."

"I know and I'm about to change that. When you told me about how you grew up with both your parents and how loving, caring and supportive they were, I thought you were the luckiest girl in the world. I never had a caring father or witnessed first-hand how a man was supposed to love and cherish his wife. Pam and I never had a daddy, we had a monster." Zoe put her fork down and dabbed her eyes with her napkin. "I witnessed him beat my mother, talk to her as if she were a dog and force himself on her whenever he took a notion. When he got tired of dealing with my mom, he turned his perversion to my sister. She suffered unspeakable acts at the hands of that man," Zoe whimpered. "And over the years, he'd promised me that my time was coming."

"Oh God, Zoe, I had no idea. I'm so sorry," April said as she choked on her tears. "I feel so stupid for all the stuff I said in the car."

"It's okay April. You had no idea about my past. I'm only telling you because I didn't want you to think I was crazy or over reacting like some crazed woman."

"I can't imagine being raped by my father. How do you recover from that? I wouldn't know how to go on with my life."

"I thank God every day for giving me the strength to stop him before he could actually carry out the act. I still carry the sting of the bastard's hands hitting me, but he didn't take everything from me."

"Now I understand why you are so stern with what you will and won't accept from Ramon. He seems like a great guy to me, but if he ever crosses the line, I promise to help you beat his ass."

CHAPTER FOURTEEN

All of her belongings were packed and had been loaded into Ramon's work truck. He and his friend pulled out of the parking lot leaving Zoe to have some private time with her family. The Shaw women sat at the kitchen table sipping on coffee. While Zoe was excited about her move, Pam and Martha were feeling uneasy and a bit disappointed that Zoe was actually going through with her plans.

"Why are y'all looking so solemn? I'm just moving a few miles away and you know I'll be over here all the time," Zoe spoke reassuringly.

"You say that you'll come over all the time, but something tells me that you'll fall into your new life and we'll become nothing more than an afterthought." Pam could no longer keep the tears from falling and her hands were red from her nervously wringing them. Martha reached over to try and get her to relax her hands, but her efforts were useless.

"Pam, you two are the only family I've got. You could never be just an afterthought to me. I love y'all more than anything or anyone. Mama, you understand I simply want the opportunity to share in a successful, loving relationship with a man that wants to make me happy."

"Yes, baby, I do understand and I would never try to deny you that opportunity. It's just that change is always a little nerve wrecking for us. Next thing we know, Pam will be moving out to be with Alvin," Martha chuckled, trying to lighten the mood. "Then it'll just be lil old me over here. I'll probably get a cat to keep me company and the next thing you know, I'll be known as the crazy cat lady in apartment B-3." They all giggled knowing that everything Martha had just said was unfathomable. Not only was she allergic to cats, but she swore the damn things were evil.

"No worries, Mama, I'll never leave you. You're stuck with me forever more," Pam reassured.

"Hell, I hope not. I know we're a little sad right now, but I'm also proud. Proud that you girls are finding the strength to rebuild you lives. Proud that after everything you've been through you still have the courage to trust and believe in love. So no ma'am, Pam, you won't be with me forever more. Hopefully the both of you will eventually move away, marry, and give me grandbabies. Just remember that I am always here and you should never be ashamed or embarrassed to run back home to mama."

They sat and talked for a while longer, reminiscing over old days, proud of how far they'd come and their hope for the future. After an hour or so had passed, Zoe's cell phone rang. "Hey, babe," she answered cheerfully.

"We've unloaded all of your boxes and I'm sitting here alone waiting for my woman to come home," Ramon spoke with a sexy growl.

Zoe giggled like a school girl, "I'm on my way." She clicked off her phone, looked at Pam and Martha with a squinted face and announced that it was time for her to go. "I love you guys and Pam, just because I left a few clothes and shoes behind doesn't mean you're free to jump in them. Those are for the nights I decide to stay over," she said as they all rose from the table. "Oh and I want to have y'all over for dinner on Sunday."

"Are you sure that'll be okay with Ramon?" Martha asked. "I mean you're just moving in, why don't we give you a little more time to get settled in?"

"Mama, it's a week away, y'all know I'll have everything straightened out in two days. And of course he's fine with it. He knows that y'all will be coming over from time to time. He has no choice but to be fine with it, I'm the boss," Zoe laughed at her declaration.

"Yeah, okay boss lady," Pam chuckled. She finally seemed to relax into the fact that Zoe was leaving. She was no longer wringing her hands and the tears had dried. She stood along with Zoe and her mom and gave her little sister a big hug. "Make sure he treats you right Zoe, and take no crap from him."

"You already know that I'm not tolerant of foolishness. I promise I'll be fine, y'all," Zoe reassured them as she wrapped her arms around her mom. "And I'll talk to you guys a little later on and see you in a couple of days."

Pulling into the driveway, Zoe noticed what looked like pieces of paper sprinkled on the front porch. As she got out and walked to the door she realized that those pieces of paper were actually white and red rose petals. With a broad smile on her face, she unlocked the door and stepped in onto a bed of rose peddles. "Ramon, I'm home." She liked the way that rolled off her tongue. Before she could repeat herself, Ramon walked up to her, removed her purse from her shoulder, and took her jacket. Holding her hand he led her back to the bedroom, undressed her, and walked her into the bathroom where there was a hot, bubble bath waiting on her. Ramon helped her into the tub, pushed play on iHome, and walked out of the room.

Zoe sat looking at the door for a moment wondering why he hadn't uttered a word. But then she figured he was trying to play the silent romantic role so she laid back and let the water wash over her. She had totally gotten lost in the music and was a little startled when Ramon kissed her forehead.

"Are you ready?" he asked softly.

"Ready for what?"

"For your bath," he said as he lathered a loofa and began to slowly bathe her body. He washed every inch of her in an incredibly seductive manner. When he was done, he helped her stand to her feet, wrapped her in a towel, and lifted her out of the tub. Ramon went on to dry her off, lotion her body, and drape her in a short, sexy chemise.

"I could get used to this kind of treatment," Zoe whispered and she wrapped her arms around Ramon and leaned in for a kiss. The light peck quickly escalated with Zoe slipping her tongue into his mouth. Ramon kissed her deeply as he allowed his hands to roam over her body. His touch was driving her crazy. She moaned as his fingers grazed her nipples and greeted him with wetness when his hand ventured over her round bottom and played between her legs. "Umm, baby, I want you so bad right now," she whispered.

Ramon laid her on the bed of the dimly lit room and quickly walked out. But to her pleasant surprise, he returned just as quickly with a tray of strawberries, chocolate, and champaign. "Cheers to us, babe," he said as they clinked glasses and drank to their new beginning. He sat the glasses down and turned his attention back to the beautiful woman lying in his bed. He kissed Zoe passionately and the sexy little gown he'd just draped her in was almost torn from her body. Ramon took her breast in his mouth, sucking and teasing her nipple with his tongue. He went from one to the other, sucking, biting, and licking as Zoe moaned with pleasure. Trailing southward, he teased her as he licked the inside of her thighs and finally he began to lick and gently suck her clit. He tasted her wetness and it made him hungry for more. Zoe arched her back and had her first orgasm of the night with Ramon drinking it in as if it were the sweetest nectar he'd ever tasted. When he entered her it took her breath away. He moved forcefully in and out and she matched him stroke for stroke until they collapsed in complete satisfaction.

CHAPTER FIFTEEN

April walked out of the credit union ready to go home and relax after a long day of dealing with argumentative customers. To her surprise, Desi was standing outside of his car waving her over. She hurried on over and greeted him with a hug. "What are you doing here, handsome?" She asked with a smile.

"I was hoping to convince you and Zoe to join me for a drink," he responded as he stroked her hair. It was impossible for Desi to hide how much he admired April's beauty. He knew without a doubt that he was gay, but it was just something about that woman.

"After a day like today, I'm more than happy to join you. A good stiff drink is the perfect way to unwind, but I can't speak for Zoe. That girl still has stars in her eyes and usually runs straight home."

As Zoe exited the building she saw her two best friends chatting and signaling for her to join them. "Hey, Desi, what are doing here?" She questioned as she threw her arms around his neck and kissed him on the cheek.

"I came to take you and April out for a drink. It's been a while and thought it'd be nice to catch up with my favorite girls."

"Aww man, I'd love to," Zoe exclaimed. "But I've got to run home and cook. Ramon is always so hungry when he gets in from work."

"Come on, Zoe, you cook for him all the time. That man can live without your Spam and instant potatoes for one day," April said sarcastically. It was everything Desi could do to not burst out laughing. The fact that Zoe couldn't really cook was no secret.

"So it's like that, y'all are going to dog out my cooking now? That's cold."

"Okay seriously Zoe, I hardly get to see you anymore. In the three months that you've lived with Ramon I've seen you twice. I mean damn, we used to spend time together at least twice a week. Is a couple hours of your time really too much to ask for now?" Desi looked at her with his puppy dog eyes, patiently awaiting her answer.

Zoe tilted her head to the side, smiled broadly and replied, "Where are we going?"

"That's my girl," Desi sang out as he planted a kiss on her forehead. "We'll head over to Tin Lizzy's, their drinks are good and you'll be able to get those fried jalapenos you love so much."

"Sounds like a plan. I'll follow you guys over there," Zoe said.

"You know that both of y'all can just ride with me. I'll bring you back to your cars when we leave the restaurant," Desi offered.

"No, Tin Lizzy's isn't that far from the house so it makes more sense for me to drive there instead of doubling back."

"Yeah, I think I'll drive too, Desi," April added.

The threesome formed a caravan and headed across town. After a ten minute wait, they were seated at a high top table and the first round of drinks were placed before them. They raised a toast to friendship, love, and life. "Well, I'll drink to two of those," April laughed. "We all know that there's no love in my life right now, but I want to hear all about y'alls. Desi, you and Kirk all good now, ironed out all the issues and concerns?"

"As a matter of fact we did and you ladies will be the first to hear this tid bit of news, we have decided to get married."

"What!" Zoe exclaimed. "Are you serious? How did you and Kirk go from fighting like cats and dogs to wanting to get married?"

"We talked and once again I reassured Kirk that I was not, nor had I ever cheated on him. He said I was welcome to come back home under the condition that I agree to couples counseling."

"You agreed to counseling?" Zoe asked in disbelief. "You've always said that the only way you'd visit a shrink was if they paid you."

"I know, but I wasn't ready to give up on Kirk and me so I was willing to try just about anything. Anyway, we went to a few sessions, talked things out and came to a mutual understanding. And you know that he recently changed jobs?"

"No, I didn't know that," Zoe said.

"I did," April boasted as if she had one up on Zoe.

"Wait a minute, how did you know before me?" Zoe questioned.

"Because she actually has time to talk to me these days," Desi said bluntly. "Now back to my story. The benefits on Kirk's job are outstanding, but his company doesn't recognize domestic partners as dependents and therefore won't insure them. So with me losing my benefits soon, Kirk had the bright idea that we run off to a State that recognizes gay marriage and then his company will have to cover me as his spouse."

"Are y'all absolutely positive about that?" April asked.

"No, but when Kirk threw it out there as a good reason to marry, I thought what the hell, it's worth a shot. Plus I knew that benefits had very little to do with anything. Kirk just really wanted us to marry, he wants to know that I belong to him."

Again, they raised their glasses in a toast. And as the evening went on, they laughed, talked about the good, bad and ugly of their lives and drank to just about anything. When asked if she still liked living with Ramon, Zoe gave a resounding yes and they drank to that too. Finally amidst the laughter and drinking, April looked at her watch and realized that it was 9:30pm. "OMG, do y'all realize what time it is? We have to get up for work in the morning and as beautiful as I am, I need my beauty rest."

"Wow, I didn't realize it had gotten so late," Zoe said as she glanced at her watch. She then pulled her purse from the back of her chair and retrieved her cell phone. Foolishly she'd forgotten to take if off of vibrate and had missed six calls from Ramon. "My man's been trying to reach me, probably missing his baby," she gushed.

Desi picked up the tab, they said their goodbyes and went their separate ways. It only took Zoe about fifteen minutes to get home. To her surprise, the house was completely dark. She surmised that Ramon had stepped out for a bit as well. She fumbled with her house key and finally slid it in the lock but it wouldn't turn. She shook the doorknob, pulled the key out, double checked that it was the correct one and tried again. Still it wouldn't turn, wouldn't unlock the door. She pulled out her cell phone and called Ramon.

"Hey babe, I'm here at home but I can't get my key to work, I can't get in the house."

"Then maybe you should've answered my calls. Maybe if you'd brought your ass home like a decent woman you'd be able to get in the house," Ramon explained as he turned on the porch light and watched her through the glass that surrounded the front door.

"Ramon, stop playing. It's cold out here, I'm tired and not in the mood for silly games."

"This isn't a game, Zoe, you need to learn to bring your ass home at a decent time if you plan to live here," Ramon screamed angrily.

"Screw this and screw you," Zoe shot back. She turned and started down the walk way to her car when Ramon swung the door open and stormed after her. He grabbed her by the arm and ordered her to get in the house. Snatching her arm away, Zoe began to yell, "Who the hell do you think you are? Don't you ever grab me like that. I will not be man-handled."

Ramon looked at her as if he could strangle her with his bare hands. He took a few deep breaths to calm himself, stepped back, and began again. "Look, Zoe, I'm sorry for changing the lock. I was upset that you hadn't returned any of my calls and didn't let me know where you were. The longer I sat here waiting on you, the more concerned I became, but eventually the concern turned to anger. You've never just gone out and not let me know if you were going to be late."

"I don't care how upset you are with me Ramon; it is not okay for you to put your hands on me. Putting your hands on me aggressively like that is unacceptable," Zoe preached as she stood her ground, letting him know that she was not taking his actions lightly.

"I know and I'm sorry. Come on, let's go in the house and finish this conversation." Ramon extended his hand as if to say "after you." Reluctantly, Zoe walked back to the door and entered the house. Ramon closed the door behind them, took her coat and purse, and led Zoe to the kitchen. "Are you hungry?"

"No, I had dinner with April and Desi."

"So they're the reason you didn't come home or answer my calls?" Ramon badgered.

"They are not the reason Ramon. The choice was mine. It's been a long time since I spent time with my friends and I miss them. I wanted to catch up and enjoy their company. Now I'm sorry I didn't answer your calls, I forgot to switch my ringer back on after work. But you can't freak out like this every time I'm late coming home. Just like you have time with your friends, I'm going to have time with mine. From now on I will let you know in advance, but they are a part of my life that I won't be giving up."

Ramon sat right in front of Zoe, took her hands in his and looked sternly in her eyes. "After a while you'll come to realize that I'm all you need. I'm the only true friend you'll need," he advised as he squeezed her hands with far more force than he should have.

CHAPTER SIXTEEN

Zoe was excited to be spending Sunday afternoon with her mom and sister. For the first time in a long time, she was looking forward to her mom's heavy, fattening meal. Ramon had a small job that he'd promised his customer would be finished before the week was over, so he was going to meet Zoe at her mom's once he was done. This was perfect for Zoe, it would give her a chance to have some alone time with her family and speak privately without Ramon hanging on her every word.

"So tell me, Pam, how are things with you and Alvin?" Zoe asked as she poured three glasses of wine.

"Everything is really good with us. He just got a big promotion at work and decided to take me on a mini vacation to celebrate," Pam gushed. "We're heading to South Beach next week for a three day weekend."

"That's great! I swear I'd give my right arm for a break."

"Why don't you suggest to Ramon that you all take a little break?" Martha suggested.

"In all honesty Mama, I'd prefer to get away alone. I could use a little time to myself to meditate, release a little stress," Zoe confessed.

As Pam and Martha looked back and forth at one another

with concern etched across their faces, Zoe sat the glasses on the table and took a seat. Following her lead, Pam and Martha sat as well. They each took a couple of sips of wine before Pam broke the brief silence. "So tell us Zoe, is everything okay with you and Ramon? Is he treating you well or are you starting to have issues with him?"

"Everything is cool for the most part. His possessiveness is starting to drive me a little crazy, but other than that, we're all good."

"Exactly what do you mean when you say his possessiveness?" Martha inquired.

Zoe told them about his over the top reaction to her hanging out with April and Desi a couple of weeks ago. "I couldn't believe that he actually changed the lock just because I went out for a bit. Hell, if I changed the locks every time he hung out with his friends the locksmith would have to move in."

"That's just ridiculous," Pam exclaimed. She was clearly annoyed with Ramon's outrageous behavior. "Why didn't you just tell him to kiss your ass and come back here?" Clearly Pam's nervous condition had been replaced with confidence and a low tolerance for foolishness.

"That's exactly what I did," Zoe explained. "But then he came running after me, pleading for me to go in the house. Once I did he proceeded to apologize and tell me how he's the only real friend that I need. And he was squeezing my hands so tight. It was all a little too weird for me and left me feeling uneasy. I still don't like the way any of that went down."

"And what did he bring you as a make-up gift the next day?" Martha asked with a stone face.

"Mama, how did you know he bought me a gift?" Zoe challenged.

"Zoe, that's a classic sign of an abuser. Baby, they treat you like crap, curse you, grab you, and eventually beat you, and they always come back with a gift," Martha spat angrily. "I want you to leave him Zoe. Come back home before he starts to escalate this behavior."

"Mama, calm down. You know I would never fall for any mess like that and I don't think that Ramon is an abuser. That was the first incident of that nature. Believe me, I stood my ground and laid down the law. I was very clear with what I would and would not accept."

"That all sounds good Zoe, but we all know that if Ramon is in fact an abuser, your laying down the law means absolutely nothing. And we know from experience that the longer you stay, the worse the behavior will get," Pam warned. "You need to bring your ass home."

"Look, y'all really do need to calm down," Zoe demanded. She looked at her mom and saw that tears were dancing at the rim of her eyes, threatening to fall down her face. "Mama please don't cry. I promise y'all that the man has never hit me and he won't. If he ever tried, he'd have one hell of a fight on his hands and I wouldn't hesitate to pack my things and come right back home."

"I'm going to trust that you'll actually do that Zoe. I pray that you're right, that he isn't an abusive man, but please don't ignore the signs. Promise me that if something like that happens again, you'll leave," Martha begged.

"I promise, Mama. Now let's finish up dinner so that it'll be ready when he and Alvin get here," Zoe suggested.

"They're getting a free meal so if they have to wait a little bit for it then oh well," Pam asserted, clearly still angry about the information her sister had just divulged.

Alvin was the first to arrive. He came in with a warm smile and comforting hugs for everyone. He couldn't help but notice the serious faces plastered on each of the women. "Is everything okay?" He asked although he had a sinking feeling that it wasn't.

"Everything is fine," Zoe assured him. "I hope you're hungry because Mama threw down today."

"I am starving! All I've had today was a cup of coffee and a protein bar. Whoever said that crap would keep you full for hours lied," Alvin laughed, but noticed that Zoe was the only one to laugh with him. "Okay ladies, for real now, what's wrong? Ms. Martha, you look like you're about to burst into tears and Pam, you act as if you're ready to punch someone's lights out. What gives?"

"It seems that Zoe is having a bit of problem with Ramon," Pam spat. "He's acting like he wants to start man handling folks and" The doorbell interrupted Pam mid-sentence.

"Look y'all, I want you to lose the attitudes right now. I don't want Ramon to know that I spoke to y'all about this. It was one incident that I don't want to cause me more problems because y'all can't get and keep your attitudes in check. Now get it together," Zoe demanded as she went and opened the front door. "Hey, baby," she said as she greeted Ramon with a hug and kiss.

"Hey, you okay? I thought I heard someone fussing in here."

"Oh no, must have been the folks in the apartment next door," Zoe lied.

Ramon stepped further into the apartment and greeted everyone with a cheerful hello. He felt as if he was greeted half-heartedly by everyone except Zoe. Thinking that it may have just been in his head, he walked over to Ms. Martha and gave her a big hug. Normally she would wrap him up into a big hug and talk sweetly to him as if he were her son. But her weak pat on the back greeting assured him that it wasn't in his head. This was a feeling that Ramon didn't like and he began to rack his brain as to why he was getting the cold shoulder. Then it hit him like a ton of bricks, Zoe must've relayed the events of the night they'd argued.

Trying to honor her sister's request, Pam attempted to straighten her face and lighten her tone. "So, Ramon, were you able to complete the job?"

"With a little help from a friend I was. I thought I was going to have to leave it until tomorrow, but a buddy of mine was nice enough to bring me the other materials I needed to go ahead and wrap it up."

"Good for you. Well I hope you're hungry because the rest of us are starving," Pam went on to say. "So guys, go wash up and we'll put plates on the table."

Alvin and Ramon did as they were instructed and when they returned to the family room, the folding table was being topped with platters of loaded baked potatoes, grilled salmon, asparagus, and Martha's delicious yeast rolls. Ramon went into the kitchen to grab the pitchers of tea and lemonade and place them on the table along with the food. Everyone took their seat and Martha began to lead them in prayer. She thanked God not only for the food, but for the protection of her family and for them to be surrounded with love and understanding. Ramon lifted his eyes slowly as everyone said amen. Platters were passed and plates were filled, but Ramon had to speak up about the cloud hanging over the table, he knew if he didn't he wouldn't be able to enjoy his meal.

"From the tension looming over the room I can only assume that Zoe told you all about our disagreement the other week," Ramon began. "I know that I was totally out of line and I've apologized for it."

"Ramon, it sounds like you were a little more than out of line," Martha interjected. "Is this your normal behavior when someone does something you don't like?"

"Absolutely not, Ms. Martha. I know that this is not an excuse, but I got really scared that Zoe was leaving me. In my mind I thought that if she wants to leave she can, but she won't be coming back in here to snatch her stuff like a thief in the night. She was going to have to talk to me and explain why. I didn't even explain to you, Zoe, just how scared I was that night. Seems that everyone I truly love has always been taken from me or voluntarily left. I guess that was my very stupid way of protecting myself from being hurt. But I swear to you that I will never hurt your daughter, Ms. Martha. I will never raise a hand to hit her, never disrespect her, and never intentionally cause her harm. I swear."

Zoe reached over and lovingly took Ramon's hand. His heartfelt speech was not only reassuring to her, but to Martha as well. Pam, on the other hand, was still giving him the side eye as if to say she wasn't totally convinced. But after Alvin gave her a gentle squeeze under the table, she relaxed her look and decided to give him the benefit of the doubt.

The evening went on with everyone enjoying the meal and the Red Velvet cake Martha made for dessert. They talked about current events, each other's jobs, and future plans. Ramon's bravery in speaking up seemed to have given almost everyone a new level of comfort and trust.

CHAPTER SEVENTEEN

There was nothing Pam loved more than spending time with her man, Alvin. He made her feel secure and loved. They had enjoyed a fun filled day of competition at Dave & Buster's and had plans to meet Zoe and Ramon for a nice dinner at McCormick & Schmick's. Although Pam still wasn't a fan of Ramon's, she was tolerant of him for her sister's sake. Pam would put up with just about anyone if it meant spending more time with Zoe. She wouldn't allow her distrust of Ramon to place a strain on her relationship with her baby sister.

They were already seated when Ramon and Zoe entered the restaurant hand in hand. They looked happy and that was pleasing to Pam. "Hey guys, it's good to see y'all," Pam sang as she and Alvin rose to their feet to greet their dinner companions.

"Hey, yourself," Ramon replied as he hugged Pam and gave a manly pat on the back to Alvin.

"Hi, sis, how are you tonight?" Zoe asked with a kiss for Pam and a warm hug for Alvin.

"I'm doing great! Alvin and I have enjoyed a fantastic day together," Pam boasted. We went to Dave & Buster's and I felt like a kid running around that game room and beating Alvin at every game we played.

"Hold on now woman, tell the story right. I let you beat me at one game of basketball," Alvin corrected.

"Humph, I could have sworn I beat you at basketball, air hockey, oh and that racing game."

"Y'all see what happens when I allow this woman to think that she can beat me? She gets carried away and thinks she's the champion of everything," Alvin laughed as he planted a tender kiss on her cheek.

"Alright, love birds; this is getting too sappy for me. I'm officially changing the topic," Zoe declared. "How was Mama today? I spoke with her briefly, but she seemed to be rushing me off the phone."

"That's because she was running around trying to clean up before she headed out for the day," Pam replied.

"Where was she going?" Zoe asked, surprised that her mom was venturing out on a Saturday without either of them.

"I introduced Ms. Martha to my mom a couple of weeks ago and they really hit it off," Alvin said. "My mom is part of a social group and she invited Ms. Martha to hang out with them today and she accepted. So your mom is at the Alliance Theatre enjoying some play and then they were heading out to dinner."

"Oh my goodness, that is so good. I'm really glad that Mama is getting a little social life of her own. Hey, babe, maybe we can introduce our parents too. Do you think your mom would enjoy hanging out with the other ladies?" Zoe inquired.

Ramon's facial expression changed from joyful to serious. "Zoe, you've only met my parents once, what makes you think that they would now want to become best friends with your family? I thought it was obvious that they're not the outgoing, fun loving types."

"Dang, babe, you don't have to get all defensive or upset, I was just asking. And how am I supposed to know what your folks are like? I met them once for five minutes, damn."

The death stare that Ramon was throwing at Zoe made everyone at the table uncomfortable. Alvin tried to change the conversation, but no matter what he talked about, the mood around the table was forever changed. Every bit of joy and light heartedness was destroyed by Ramon's over-reaction.

"So, are you guys coming to dinner tomorrow?" Pam asked. "Mama is cooking her famous roast."

"We can't make it," Ramon blurted out before Zoe could form an answer on her lips.

Zoe looked at Ramon with annoyance written all over her face. "Why can't we make it?"

"I promised my friend that we'd swing by his house for the game and a little dinner. And I volunteered you for dessert. So you need to come up with something tasty."

Again, Alvin tried to lighten the mood and jokingly told Zoe that she might be better off buying something from the bakery. Everyone gave a little smile, but for Ramon it was the funniest thing that had been said all night.

"He may have a point, babe. Hard as you try, you can't cook worth a damn," Ramon laughed uncontrollably. After realizing that no one else saw the humor in his comment, he tried to defend his joke. "So now everyone can tease and laugh about your cooking but me?"

"You know, Ramon, it's the way in which you do it. Your jokes are delivered in a manner that's meant to be hurtful. It doesn't come off as a joke, but rather a stab. You need to check your delivery, make sure your little jokes aren't taken the wrong way," Pam confronted.

"It's cool Pam. I knew he was joking," Zoe said with a half-smile.

Only a few meaningless words were shared the rest of the evening. As soon as everyone was finished eating, Ramon asked for the check, immediately gave the waitress his credit card, and waited impatiently for her return. Five minutes later she placed the receipt on the table; he signed it, stood up and held his hand out for Zoe. "Come on, time for us to call it a night."

Pam gave her sister a big hug and kiss, the she whispered in her ear, "You can always come home."

"I know, but really I'm all good." She kissed Pam and gave Alvin a hug goodbye.

Ramon took Zoe's hand in his and they walked out the restaurant looking like a happy couple. Zoe couldn't help but think about how funny it was that appearances can be so different from reality. At that very moment the two of them were anything but happy. Zoe was pissed and embarrassed by Ramon's behavior and she wanted to know why he felt the need to speak to her the way he had. They crossed the street and walked through the parking deck in silence, but once they exited the lot, Zoe tore into him.

"What the hell was that, Ramon? Why did you speak to me like that? All I did was suggest that we introduce our parents and you jumped all over me like I tried to kill you. It was disrespectful and uncalled for."

"If you want me to talk to you, you better check your damn tone. You ain't gonna talk to me any old kind of way. And if you call that bitch my mother one more time, I swear you'll regret it. They are my adoptive parents, understand...adoptive!"

"Whatever, Ramon! The point is that all I was trying to do was bring our families together and make decent dinner conversation. But you just don't know how to let people be happy in your presence. And don't forget that you're the one that bragged about how close you and your mother were. Make up your mind, either y'all are close or she's a bitch. I swear sometimes you act like you were raised by wolves instead of parents."

Without warning, Ramon extended his hand and popped Zoe in the mouth. She covered her mouth and stared at him in a state of shock. But after what he'd just done sank in, Zoe balled up her fist and whacked him in his face. "Don't you ever put your damn hands on me," she screamed as she continued to pummel him. "I am not your punching bag!" Ramon managed to pull the car over and tried to hold Zoe's hands to prevent her from landing another punch, but when that didn't work; he drew back and punched her in the nose. Zoe screamed in agony and blood flowed like a waterfall.

"See what you made me do," Ramon shouted as he scrambled for napkins to hold up to her nose. "Baby, I'm sorry, but what was I supposed to do, let you beat my ass?" He managed to change the tone of his voice to try and convey sincerity and regret. "I'm so sorry, babe. Do you want me to drive you to the hospital?"

"Drive me home," Zoe answered in a cold voice as she held her head back to try and stop the bleeding.

"Babe, you have to know that I didn't mean it. I didn't mean to hurt you. I just wanted you to stop hitting me. I swear, babe, I'm so sorry."

"Take me home now!" Zoe demanded

Ramon finally pulled into the drive. Zoe jumped out of the car and ran into the house with Ramon hot on her heels. He was still trying to apologize, but she was not interested in anything he had to say. While he talked, she packed. She filled her overnight bag with only the necessities, grabbed her purse and keys, and headed towards the door.

"Babe, please don't leave me," Ramon begged. "I love you so much and I'll do anything to make this up to you. Please just don't leave me."

"You promised me and my family that you'd never lay hands on me in a violent way. You lied and I have no reason to believe that you won't do it again. I've told you about my past, how I grew up, yet you still punched me in the face like I'm some dude on the street."

"I messed up big time, Zoe and I know that. I just wanted you to stop hitting me, but I went about it the wrong way." Ramon dropped to his knees and with tears rolling down his cheeks, he begged, "I'll do anything you want if you would just stay."

Zoe tried to walk out the door, but her heart just wouldn't

let her. She rationalized that had she not became violent with him, he wouldn't have laid his hands on her. "I need to know that this will never happen again."

"It won't, Zoe, I swear it won't."

"Your words mean nothing to me, Ramon. Prove it by going to counseling with me and taking an anger management class on your own."

"If that's what it takes then I'll go. We can find someone on the internet tonight and I'll call and make an appointment tomorrow."

"No, I'll find someone from a list of providers that accept my insurance and schedule our first appointment myself. But please know that if you fail to complete anger management or fail to show up for our counseling sessions, I'll be out of here… for good."

CHAPTER EIGHTEEN

After calling out sick for the past two days, Zoe wasn't surprised that April was calling. She'd called yesterday, but Zoe just wasn't ready to talk to anyone, wasn't ready to start lying in order to cover up the truth. But she knew that if she didn't answer the phone today, her family and friends would literally start knocking the door down trying to find out what was going on. So she took a deep breath and answered, "Hello."

"Hey girl, are you okay? I've been calling you for two days now. Why haven't you come to work?"

"I've been a little under the weather the last couple of days. Between menstrual cramps and fighting off a cold, I just wasn't up for work, but I'll be in tomorrow."

"Well you should've let me know. I've really been worried about you. So much so that if you didn't answer the phone this time, I was going to call Desi so that he could do a drive by with me. We were going to be over there banging on your door."

"Come on now girl, no need for all that, I'm fine. Have I missed anything major at work?"

"Not at all, just the usual crap. But without you being here the days seem to be moving a lot slower. Do you need me to drop by with anything, you know, soup or tissues?"

"Thanks for the offer, but Ramon has already gotten me both. I'm going to go in here and get a little more rest so I'll be ready for work tomorrow."

"Alright, well if you need anything you know you can call me day or night."

"I know and I appreciate that, April. Thanks a million." Zoe said goodbye and went back to watching *The Steve Harvey Show*. Watching television, eating junk food, and laying around was all that Zoe had done for the last couple of days. She didn't want to be seen by anyone because there was still some slight bruising around her nose. She hadn't been in the mood to explain and lie about what happened. So she chose to become a temporary recluse. The time alone, peace, quiet, and rest had actually felt really good. She just hated the way it had come about. Ramon, sensing that the best thing he could do was to leave her alone, had made himself scarce. He'd been leaving early, working late, and keeping quiet. But Zoe knew that his mousy behavior was going to be short lived.

Just as she'd predicted, Ramon had returned to his normal behavior. He didn't work late, but instead came home at his usual time and his first question was what's for dinner? Zoe looked at him as if he were talking gibberish. She turned her attention back to the TV because her favorite 80's show, *A Different World*, was now on. "Babe, did you hear me? What's for dinner?" Ramon asked again.

"I don't know, I assumed you were going to pick something up on your way in," she responded without ever turning her attention from the television.

"But we just went grocery shopping less than a week ago. The fridge and cabinets are full of food, so why would I pick up take out?"

"Because I didn't want to cook. These two days have been my recovery and relaxation days," Zoe answered with a touch of defiance in her voice.

"So you haven't done a thing today." Ramon was clearly disgusted.

"Oh, but I did do something. I made your appointment with a therapist for anger management. You'll have eight sessions staring tomorrow evening at 6:00pm. I got you the latest appointment they had. I also scheduled us for four couple's therapy sessions. We'll do those on the days that you don't have anger management." Zoe watched Ramon closely to see if his facial expression would change to one of anger. To her pleasant surprise, he remained calm and unaffected.

"Okay, just text me the address of the therapist so I'll have it in my phone. What day do we go to the first couple's session?"

"Friday evening and I figured we could leave there and go out for a nice dinner. Is that cool with you?" Zoe asked.

"That's fine, but what are we going to do about dinner tonight? I swear I'm about to starve."

Zoe looked at him and took into consideration that he had been working hard all day. "The best I can offer is chili dogs and fries."

"I'll take it," he replied as he made his way to the bedroom to undress and wash the days stress away in a hot shower.

As the water poured over him, he couldn't help but focus on how annoyed he was becoming with Zoe. Yes, he had agreed to the therapy, he would've agreed to just about anything to keep Zoe from walking out the door. But now he felt that she was taking all of this a tad too far. He reasoned that she never would've gotten popped in the nose if she hadn't been trying to beat up on him. Hell, as far as he was concerned she needed to be in anger management as well. And if she didn't stop sitting around moaning about recovering and healing as if she'd been shot, he was going to scream. Ramon finished his shower, threw on some sweats and sat on the side of the bed to try and decompress before going back out to deal with Zoe.

"Babe, dinner is ready," Zoe yelled out.

Even though she was serving a less than gourmet meal, she

decided to at least serve it with a little flare. When Ramon walked into the kitchen, he found candles burning, soft music playing, and his meal served on their so called good china. A smile spread across his face and he was relieved that there would be no more cold shoulder or rehashing of Saturday night's events. For him, this was a sign that Zoe was finally ready to let it go and move on.

"These are the best chili dogs ever, babe."

"I think you're just hungry. So tell me, how was your day? Did you get that house renovation job you were bidding on?"

"As a matter of fact I did. And babe, it's going to net me about $5,000 more than I initially thought it would."

"That's great, Ramon, if you keep this up you'll have to hire a couple of more workers to keep up with demand."

"Yeah, that's the plan. If I get this other job out in Alpharetta I'll have to hire someone sooner than I had anticipated. I should know in a few days if I'll get it," he said proudly as he shoved food in his mouth.

They continued eating, talking, and laughing as if all of the issues from the past few days were behind them. Zoe was sharing the topics of the crazy talk shows she'd watched over the course of the past two days when the doorbell rang.

"Are you expecting someone?" Zoe asked.

"Yeah, Harvey's picking me up to go hang with the guys for a little bit," Ramon explained as he got up to answer the door. "Hey, dude, come on in. Grab a seat and I'll be ready in a second. Babe, you remember Harvey, right?"

"Hi, Harvey, it's nice to see you again," Zoe smiled as she rushed back to the bedroom to join Ramon. "Where are you guys headed to?"

"Just to a little club for a few. I promise I won't be long."

"Another strip club I assume."

"You know I don't pay any attention to those women. I go just to have a drink and hang with the fellas," Ramon reassured her.

"Just make sure you keep your hands and money to yourself. If you want to make it rain for anyone, let it be me," she teased. "And my dances come complete with an amazing orgasm."

She kissed Ramon deeply and again warned him to keep his hands and money in his pockets. She watched him walk out the door as she struggled to keep her disapproval of his little outing to herself.

Zoe went back to watching television when she was struck with an idea. She jumped up, showered, lotioned her body, and sprayed on her favorite fragrance. She then went through her lingerie drawer and pulled out the sexiest outfit she had. The seductive sounds of Kem played in the background and candles illuminated the room.

"Babe, I'm home. Told you I wouldn't be gone long," Ramon bellowed from the front room. "Where are you?"

"Come on back to the room, baby."

Ramon looked disgusted as he wondered if she'd already gone to bed. As he got closer, he heard the music and smelled the fragrant candles. When he saw Zoe draped across the bed in her heels, stockings, garter, and bustier his jaw hit the floor.

"Come in, let me help you relax," she offered as she crawled off the bed and helped him remove his jacket. "Have a seat, relax and enjoy the show."

Zoe changed the music to the raunchy, "Drunk In Love" song by Beyoncé and began to dance for her man. She shook her ass in his face, danced in the middle of the floor, and grinded on his lap until he felt he would explode. Ramon stood to his feet, grabbed Zoe, and threw her back on the bed. He undressed in record time and made love to her like he never had before. It was more forceful, animalistic and she loved it. She had successfully seduced her man and hopefully convinced him that there was no need for him to ever visit a strip club again.

CHAPTER NINETEEN

Sitting in the therapist's office was more than a little uncomfortable for Ramon. In his opinion he didn't have any anger problems. Everything that occurred had been precipitated by Zoe. But if this was going to make her happy and keep her in his life, then so be it. He looked across the room as the woman casually walked in and he waited for her to start so that he could get this over with.

"Mr. Martinez, I appreciate you giving me the opportunity to work with you," Dr. Lyncs said as she walked over and extended her hand.

Ramon gave her a weak handshake but didn't open his mouth to speak. He watched as she gathered her tablet and pen and took a seat directly across from him. He took notice of how pretty she was. He wasn't normally into white chicks, but for her he'd make an exception. He watched as she crossed her legs and wondered what kind of panties she was wearing, if any at all. He envisioned himself tossing her up on her desk and screwing her until she begged for mercy.

"Mr. Martinez, are you with me?" Dr. Lyncs asked as she waved her hand in front of him.

"Oh, I'm sorry. I guess my mind drifted," Ramon apologized. "And please, call me Ramon. I get nervous when people call me by my last name," he joked.

"Alright then, Ramon, care to tell me where you were drifting off to?"

"Just thinking about work," he lied.

"Well why don't you tell me what brings you here today?" She asked although she saw from her pre-appointment notes that he apparently had anger issues. But still, she needed to hear him say why he was there.

"My girlfriend thinks I need anger management," he replied bluntly.

"And what makes her think that?"

"We had an incident this past weekend where she started hitting me. When I couldn't get her to stop, I hit her in the face. I didn't mean to hit her as hard as I did, but it did stop her from beating up on me."

Dr. Lyncs jotted down a few notes. While she was writing, Ramon again drifted to thoughts of him banging her. He wondered if she liked it rough, if she was a prude in bed, or if she was even having sex at all. He heard his name and looked from her legs to her eyes.

"So, Ramon, do you think that the end justified the means?" Dr. Lyncs asked.

"What do you mean?"

"Do you think that it was okay to hit your girlfriend if it made her stop hitting you?"

"I mean, I don't think it's okay to go around hitting women and I wish I hadn't hit Zoe, but it's also not okay for a woman to beat up on a man. I'm not trying to justify what I did, but at this point it is what it is. I'm not an abusive man and I've promised her that I'll never hit her again."

"Statistically speaking, if a man is violent with his mate once, he will likely be violent again."

Ramon started looking at Dr. Lynch differently. In his eyes she started going from hot to bitchy. She hadn't said anything offensive, but her talk about statistics seemed to Ramon as if she were telling him that he was guaranteed to hit Zoe again.

"I don't really care about statistics. I said that I wouldn't hit her again and that's what I meant."

Dr. Lyncs could see and hear his rapidly growing frustration. They'd barely scratched the surface and his agitation was very apparent, so much so that she was wondering how upset might he get as they continued on. "I can tell that you're becoming a little annoyed with this situation. Is it my questions that are bothering you or the fact that you are even here?"

"Or maybe I'm annoyed because you're making assumptions about me and you've only known me for ten minutes. You and Zoe both are making me out to be some monster," he retorted.

"Why do you feel like we're making you out to be a monster? That wasn't my intention."

"If Zoe weren't trying to make me out to be some crazed man I wouldn't be here. One incident and she gives me the ultimatum of therapy or she leaves me. You're supposed to be a neutral party and yet you've already accused me of hitting her again. Why the hell wouldn't I be agitated? This is all bullshit and you know it."

"I didn't accuse you Ramon. And it's not my intention to upset you. I'm sorry that you feel you've been unfairly judged. The purpose of this is to help you better control your anger so that you won't repeat the behavior."

"There you go again, it's not a behavior. A behavior is something that's been repeated, I hit the bitch once," Ramon spat angrily. "That's what's wrong with y'all, always trying to fix somebody when y'all ain't got the common sense it takes to comprehend basic shit."

"Who is y'all?" Dr. Lyncs asked.

"Don't play stupid with me. Y'all as in women, the only people that are so smart you're stupid. Think you know everything and you really know nothing!" Ramon was furious.

"You seem to have a very distorted view of women. Do you

really believe that the entire gender is stupid?" she asked more out of curiosity. She also hoped that if she gave him a chance to vent it would help to calm him down. She was wrong.

"Every time you open your mouth you prove that my father was right. He's the one that explained to me how brain dead y'all are. I tried my best not to believe him, but damn it, y'all keep proving him right. What kind of idiot thinks they can beat up on somebody and not get knocked the hell out? And you sitting here making assumptions and accusations and don't expect for it to upset me," Ramon continued on his rant. But when he realized that the therapist was jotting down all kinds of notes again, he completely lost it. He jumped from his seat and snatched the note pad out of her hand before she realized what was happening.

"Mr. Martinez, I'm going to need for you to calm down." Despite her efforts to hide it, Dr. Lyncs was clearly shaken.

"Everything you've written is crap and I don't have time for this bullshit. Thanks for nothing." Ramon stormed out of the office with no intentions to ever go back.

An hour later, Ramon had called his boy, Rich, and they were bellied up to the bar throwing back shots. Ramon was still angry. Angry with the therapist and with Zoe for giving him such a ridiculous ultimatum in the first place. But most of all, he was pissed with himself for not handling Zoe in a manner that would have prevented all this in the first place. He now realized that he'd given her too much freedom, too much input, and clearly hadn't been stern enough with her from the beginning of their relationship. Like his dad used to say, treat them like the simple minded kids they are and you won't have to worry about reining them in later.

"So what do you plan to do about Zoe now? How will you tell her that you're not going back to therapy?" Rich asked.

"I'm not telling her anything. As far as I'm concerned she can continue to think that I'm going." Ramon threw back another shot.

"Dude, you better handle that. You can't let these women rule you. Hell, I know you're not scared of her, so put your foot down, handle your business, and tell her you're not going back. You are the man and ruler of that house, now make her ass fall in line," Rich offered his unsolicited advice.

"You're right; I'm tired of bowing down and caving to her ridiculous demands. It's time for Zoe to fall in line and I'll do whatever I have to to make her."

Across town, Zoe had stopped by Martha and Pam's place to say hello and catch up. She hated she'd missed Sunday dinner, but there was no way she was going to let them see her with that bruised face.

"Hey Mama, how are you?" Zoe asked as she kissed her mother hello.

"I'm fine, sweetheart, how are you? And why haven't I seen you in over a week?"

"I'm fine and I'm sorry I hadn't gotten over here before now. I wasn't feeling my best earlier this week and actually took a couple of days off just to recoup. Where is Pam?"

"That girl just got out the shower and is getting dressed. She had a late night and is moving in slow motion today. What was wrong with you? Did you go see a doctor? You should've called me and I would have come by after work to cook you some soup or something." Martha was always overly concerned for her daughters and was now giving Zoe the once over to make sure that she couldn't see anything visibly wrong with her.

"No, I didn't need a doctor Mama, it was just a stomach bug," she lied. "And I didn't want to bother you. Besides, Ramon took great care of me," she assured as the lies continued to fall from her lips.

"Hey, chicka!" Pam bounced out of her room and went straight to Zoe for a big hug. When she stepped back from her sister, she noticed a small dark mark just under Zoe's eye. "What happened to your eye, did Ramon punch you?" Pam chuckled at her little joke, never realizing that she'd hit the nail right on the head.

"Ha-ha, very funny, Pam. I actually clocked myself with the cabinet door the other day. That thing hurt like hell, but thankfully didn't leave a real bad bruise." Zoe hated how the lies were piling up. She, Pam, and Martha had always been one hundred percent honest with one another and now all of that was changing. But at least Ramon was getting the help she thought he needed and she'd never have to repeat these kinds of lies to her family again.

CHAPTER TWENTY

Tonight was the last night of Ramon and Zoe's couple's therapy. For the most part things had been going fine. They hadn't argued, had both been open and honest about their abusive pasts, and Zoe was sure that Ramon now understood how important it was to her that violence not be a part of their relationship. The therapy also helped her to understand her role in the punching incident. She apologized for first hitting him and vowed that she would find a better way to express her anger. But as the session was coming to an end, the therapist asked a question that turned everything upside down.

"You guys have made great progress in this short amount of time. Just remember all the coping tools you learned here and you should be fine. Ramon, how is the anger management coming along? You should only have a couple more sessions of that, right?"

"In all honesty, Dr. Faulkner, I haven't been back since the first session," he said bluntly.

Zoe was shocked and confused. "You told me that the therapy was going well. And if you haven't been going to your sessions then where have you been spending that time?"

"Look, I'm sorry I lied, but I didn't care for Dr. Lyncs. It's like she had her mind made up about me before she ever met me. That chick immediately started telling me how I was likely to hit you again and again, making assumptions about me and didn't even know me. I knew then that that was a waste of my time. Besides, we've had this therapy and its worked fine."

"Ramon, this is different from the anger management. While it pleases me that you've gotten so much from this type of therapy, I strongly encourage you to seek out another therapist for anger management. I actually think that a male therapist is more appropriate for that anyway. I'd be glad to make a couple of suggestions," Dr. Faulkner offered.

"Thanks, but no thanks," Ramon replied sternly. "This is all the head shrinking that I need. Besides, all I did was defend myself against her abuse," he asserted as he pointed at Zoe.

"Are you serious? You punched me in my freaking nose like we were dudes in a damn street fight. I lost two days of work and lied to my family and friends to cover up for that crap. To cover for you!" Zoe exclaimed. She made no effort to hide her anger.

"Look, you both have made good progress here, let's not throw it all out the window now," Dr. Faulkner said as she tried to bring calm back to the room. "Ramon, do you really believe that you'll be able to deal with this relationship without raising a hand to her again?"

"Why aren't you asking her that? She hit me first. Now I love Zoe and want us to be together, but I don't understand why I'm viewed as the only abusive one in this relationship."

"The past abuse that both of you suffered and witnessed is concerning to me. And while you may not have liked Dr. Lyncs' approach, I'm sure that all she was trying to convey was that men, more so than women, tend to turn to violence."

"See, this is what I have a problem with, y'all women sticking together. Even when I didn't initiate this shit, y'all want to blame it all on me and assume that whipping her ass is going to become a routine part of our relationship."

"Oh, I'm not worried about that," Zoe spat. "Because you have one more time to lay a hand on me and I'm out. I didn't allow my father to continue with his abuse and I be damned if I'll allow you to abuse me. I love you, Ramon, but the fact that you've been lying to me for weeks is a problem. If it's been so easy for you to lie about therapy, what else do I have to worry about, what else have you been lying about? Why should I believe that you won't hit me again?" Zoe's anger had turned to tears. She cried because she was hurt, she cried because she loved Ramon, and she cried because she knew that this was not how things were supposed to be.

"Babe, please don't cry. I hate to see you cry and swear that I'll never lie to you again. I'll never raise my hand in violence to you. You've got to believe me, babe, I love you," Ramon confessed.

"Look guys, I'm glad that your love for one another is so strong, but I believe that we need to continue this for a few more weeks. Especially if you're not going to participate in anger management. I want to see you two succeed as a couple and I think that you will if you continue to seek counsel."

Ramon's first thought was 'hell no' but he knew that if he said that, things would only get worse and Zoe would probably go home and pack. He did love Zoe and that's why he agreed to a few more sessions, but once they got away from Dr. Faulkner, he'd do his best convince Zoe that counseling was no longer necessary. But for now, a smile and a nod is what he gave them, but that's all he would give them. He wouldn't give another second of his time for this bullshit counseling.

On the way home, Ramon decided to swing by Sweet Georgia's Juke Joint and treat Zoe to a good meal. The live band was always good and the atmosphere was festive. He figured that this would be a good way to move on and hopefully forget about that therapy crap. The place was full and the hostess asked if they had a reservation. But after Ramon slipped her a twenty, they were seated at the next available table. The band was already playing and he watched Zoe as she swayed to the beat of the music. A couple of glasses of wine, a good meal, and soothing music worked like a charm. By the time they were ready to leave, Zoe was all hugged up to him and playing kissy face. Despite the way it started, he knew that this night would end on a good note.

* * *

"So to what do we owe this treat?" Desi and April took a seat at the bar in Zoe's kitchen as she went about the business of serving up the pizza she'd ordered for them. "You haven't had us over in for never," Desi said laughing hysterically at his own corny joke.

"Here we go with the jokes," Zoe smirked. "You know y'all are my people and I wanted to spend some time with you guys. Y'all know I love you."

"We love you too Zoe but I was starting to wonder if you were homeless," April continued to tease. "I thought your house with Ramon was a figment of your imagination or something."

"Okay, I get it and I'm sorry. I haven't had y'all over and I know I haven't spent much time with either of you. In all honesty, Ramon and I had some things to work through, but we're all good now. I guess I just didn't really want to be around anyone until I had completely adjusted to my living situation. Now, who wants wine?"

"We both want wine," Desi said as he stood to open the wine bottle for Zoe and fill the goblets. "Where are we eating, at the bar or the table?"

"Let's eat at the table so that we can see one another without having to turn all around." Zoe placed the plates on the table. "Do you guys want the parmesan and red pepper flakes for your pizza?"

Before anyone could answer, they heard the front door open and close. Ramon walked in, peeked in the kitchen and turned to head to the bedroom. He never opened his mouth or acknowledged anyone in any way. Once he crossed the threshold to the bedroom, he began to disrobe, headed for the bathroom and turned on the shower. Zoe excused herself for a moment and went into the bedroom to see what was going on. She entered the room and quietly closed the door.

"Hey, babe, are you okay? You came in and didn't speak to me or our guests. Are you feeling alright?"

"It's been a long day Zoe and instead of coming home to a quiet home and a nice meal, I walk in on you and your little queen friends. I'm not in the mood to make nice with anyone, especially them," Ramon said flatly.

"Why can't you be bothered with my friends when I tolerate yours all the time? Every time I turn around Harvey and Rich are chilling up in here like it's their house. This is the first time any of my friends have been over. Why can't you be just as gracious to mine as I am to yours? And please do not refer to Desi as a queen, its very offensive."

"This is my house and my friends are always welcome. And since this is my house, I don't have to be gracious to anyone I don't want to. Lastly, I will call that queen anything I want to, just be thankful I don't call him something worse," Ramon stepped into the shower leaving Zoe wondering what in the world brought all of this on.

"Fine, I'll go out to eat with them tonight so that we can catch up. You have clearly had a bad day and I'm going to leave you here to relax and decompress. I'll be back in a little while."

Zoe turned to leave when Ramon reached around the shower curtain and aggressively grabbed her arm. Zoe tried to snatch her arm back, but his grasp was too tight.

"No, you stay here and entertain your little friends. I'm going out to grab a beer and let you have your moment. But don't get it twisted; I'm not coming home to a house full of folks every day, so get this entertainment crap out of your system." He let her go with a little shove and ordered her to return to her company.

Zoe dried the water from her arm and eyes. Everything had been going well and now she wondered if it was all just an act to keep her there. She wiped the last tear from the corner of her eye and headed back to the kitchen. To her dismay, April and Desi were gathering their things in preparation to leave.

"What are y'all doing? Put your stuff down. Sit down and let's eat," she demanded. Zoe turned to walk into the kitchen and when she didn't see them following her lead, she again fussed like an annoyed parent. "Hello, am I talking to the wall? Come on guys."

"Zoe, we don't want to be the cause of any problems," April stated with sad eyes. "So how about we just leave and we can all hook up later this week after work?"

"No. You all sit, enjoy your meal, and catch up. Babe, I'll be back later," Ramon said as he hustled out the front door.

April hesitantly placed her things down on the sofa, "Okay, let's eat. Desi, are you going to stay?"

Desi had been standing just watching Zoe; he knew that she wasn't right. Without words, he walked over to her and wrapped her in his arms. She tried to resist his embrace, but quickly gave in, melted into his strong chest, and let the tears flow freely. It felt good to be comforted; it was like a cleansing for her heart. She hadn't been able to share her emotions over the hitting incident, therapy, or Ramon's ever changing moods. And though it felt good to be held, she still didn't think that exposing everything was a good idea. When Zoe's crying subsided, Desi ushered her into the kitchen and April followed closely behind.

"Zoe, you don't appear to be very happy right now. I know you love Ramon, but y'all seemed to be better as a couple when you lived separately," Desi said. He was never one for mincing words and didn't feel the need to start now.

"Wow, Desi, don't you think you're jumping to a lot of conclusions?" Zoe asked. "This is just one bad day for us."

"Girl, don't try to give me some snow job. I've known you practically your whole life and we've never gone more than three or four days without talking. Now that you've moved up in here, I'm lucky if I talk to you once a week. And damn if you don't sound like you've lost your best friend when we do talk. Where is your happiness? That sense of peace and joy you felt after you moved to Atlanta?"

"I still have it, Desi; it's just been an adjustment for both me and Ramon. He has his funny ways and Lord knows I have mine, but running away at the first disagreement or misunderstanding is not the way to build a lasting relationship. There are some things that we're both going to have to learn to live with."

"Look Zoe, I hear what you're saying, but keep in mind that the things you tolerate now will likely become the things that you hate later. So be sure that the crap he's giving you is what you're willing to live with for the rest of your life. If not, it may be time to reevaluate this relationship," Desi said bluntly.

"Oh, so now you just want me to abandon the relationship all together? Ramon has so many good qualities and the good definitely outweighs the bad. And who knows, with a little counseling some of the bad can be improved upon." Zoe hated the way she was sounding. Hated that she was sounding like some heart sick, weak ass woman.

"I know you're not serious?" April chimed in. "You know you can't change people, they are who they are. The most you can hope for is that they'll change their behavior and that's not likely to happen." She picked up her glass and asked, "Can I get an amen?" Desi was more than happy to shout amen.

"Great, you two ganging up on me is just what I need to feel better. I thought this was going to be a fun, lighthearted night for us, but it seems to have turned into some kind of intervention. I love y'all, but I don't think you're being fair. You've spent very little time with Ramon and it's not fair to judge him off of his behavior today. You know it's more to a person than what you see in brief snippets," Zoe said, trying to offer up a defense for her man. But in her heart she didn't know if she was trying to convince her friends or herself.

"And we love you too Zoe and all we want is the best for you. If Ramon makes you happy then so be it, we'll step back. But if anything ever goes haywire, we'll be right here for you." Desi leaned in and kissed her on the cheek as did April.

"Thank you guys. Now can we please eat, drink, and be merry?" Zoe asked as she dabbed the tears out the corner of her eyes.

CHAPTER TWENTY-ONE

It had been a rough day at work, and more than anything, Zoe wanted to spend a little time with her mother. Martha may not have been able to protect her and her sister when they were younger, but she'd always been a phenomenal comforter. And right now, that's exactly what Zoe needed. Ramon's mood swings were becoming almost unbearable. When he was loving and kind, it was wonderful. They'd laugh, play, cook together, and make amazing love. But when he was having a bad day, he was impossible to deal with. Everything she did was wrong, he'd snap, push, argue, and, God forbid, he'd want to have sex. He would make it as un-pleasurable and demeaning for her as possible. She didn't know if he would be in a good or bad mood this evening, but before finding out, she would find love and comfort in the arms of her mother.

"Hey, baby, come on back to the kitchen and talk to your mama," Martha insisted as she let go of the tight hug she'd had on Zoe.

"Where is Pam?"

"She's going out to dinner with Alvin this evening. She didn't take an overnight bag with her when she left this morning, so I'm assuming she'll be back tonight."

"I never imagined Pam would be this happy with any man, but Alvin brings so much joy to her life. I'm so happy for her," Zoe said as she took a seat at the kitchen table.

Martha poured them each a cup of tea and took a seat next to Zoe. "Yes, she is happy, baby. Are you?"

"Why would you ask me that, Mama? Don't I look happy?" Zoe asked as she tried to conjure up a sincere smile.

"Zoe, I'm your mother. I know you better than anyone and I know when my baby is not happy. That sad, little fake smile can't convince me that you've found true happiness with Ramon."

Martha sipped her tea and waited to hear what her daughter would say next. She was hoping against all hope that Zoe wasn't going to try and defend her relationship.

"Mama, what makes you think it's my bond with Ramon that's causing me to not be happy? Maybe it's my job or just the stresses of life."

"Or maybe it's the economy or the war in Iraq. Zoe, you can blame anything you want to, but I can see the truth. You are my baby and it's breaking my heart to see this new-found sadness in your eyes. You love your job as well as the people you work with and I know that hasn't changed."

Zoe's cell phone rang and she fished it out of her purse. When she saw that it was Ramon she placed it face down on the table. She wanted to have uninterrupted time with her mother. "I don't know Mama. When things are good between me and Ramon, they're really good. But when he gets in these funky moods, he's almost unbearable. I love him, but his unpredictability is a lot to handle."

Martha looked directly in Zoe's eyes and was as blunt as she could possibly be. "Has he hit you, Zoe?"

Zoe diverted her eyes and her lengthy pause provided Martha with the answer that she didn't want. Martha moved her chair closer to Zoe's and like a child, Zoe laid her head in her mother's lap and began to weep. She cried because she loved

Ramon so much, she cried for becoming the kind of woman she never wanted to be, and she cried because despite it all, she wasn't ready to leave him.

Martha stroked her baby's hair and cried silent tears. "I know you're not ready now. It's going to take something drastic for you to want to leave. But baby, I beg you, please don't wait until it's too late. I realize that you love him and that he loves you, but please don't let him love you to death." Martha's tears were no longer silent; she wasn't able to hold back the flood of emotion. Zoe was the strong one in the family and to now see her like this was almost more than Martha could take. She cried and prayed for God to protect Zoe from further hurt and harm.

Zoe's phone rang again and when she saw it was Ramon, she simply put it back in her purse, said her goodbyes to Martha, and headed home. A little while later she pulled up to the house and was annoyed to find Rich's truck parked in the driveway. She was not in the mood to deal with company, especially Rich. He was the biggest, most arrogant jackass she'd ever met. She'd only met his little mousy girlfriend, Candy, once and after ten minutes in Rich's presence she felt nothing but pity for his girlfriend. Zoe walked into the house and politely said hello, but she never broke her stride as she headed for the bedroom.

"Where you going, babe? I haven't seen you all day. Don't you want to sit out here with us and catch the end of the game?" Ramon asked.

Zoe paused for a moment. "Thanks, baby, but I'm exhausted. I think I'll just head on back and get ready for bed," she replied as she tried to continue on to the bedroom.

"Well, will you at least throw us a couple of sandwiches together before going back?"

"How long have you been home Ramon?"

"A couple of hours, why?"

"Babe, you could've prepared a full meal by now. I'm really tired and it won't take you but a minute to slap some mayo and ham on some bread." Zoe turned and went on in the room and closed the door.

"Damn, man, whose house is this? Cause it looks like she's running things. I wish the hell Candy would talk to me like that or walk out on me," Rich bellowed as if he were trying to insight a riot. He leaned back into the sofa with his round belly still sticking out as if he were eight months pregnant. His hair slicked back into a ponytail made him look as if he were some sleazy used car salesman. He kept staring at Ramon with those beady eyes waiting to see his friend's reaction.

As if he were a twelve year old, Ramon was unwilling to look like a punk in front of his friend. Without hesitation, he took off towards the bedroom. What he didn't need was more encouragement, but that slimy, no good Rich offered it anyway.

"That's right, bro. Go handle your business."

Ramon stormed into the room slamming the door behind him. Startled by the loud noise, Zoe jumped and looked around to see Ramon fuming.

"What's wrong, babe? Did something happen with you and Rich?"

"No, something happened with you. How are you gonna come up in here and embarrass me like that. You roll up in here and act like you're too good to hang out with me and my boy and then refuse to fix a couple of sandwiches. You need to get your damn clothes back on and come out here and fix us something to eat!" Ramon demanded.

"You sound like a crazy man! When my friends are here you won't even speak to them. At least I acknowledge that animal you call a friend. And y'all are grown ass men perfectly capable of fixing a sandwich. I'm going to bed. Goodnight!" Zoe shouted as she slipped her shoes off. But Ramon walked up on her and grabbed her by the arm. He dug his nails into her flesh so hard that she immediately began to bruise, and when she still seemed unwilling, he dug in until he drew blood. "Ramon, I swear if you don't let me go I'm calling the cops," she threatened, trying her best not to cry.

"What you're going to do is take your ass out there, fix us something to eat, and act like you're glad to do it." He never let go of her arm as he shuffled her out of the room and into the kitchen. As they passed by Rich, they could hear him shouting words of encouragement to Ramon.

"So you're treating me like this to try and impress that fool?" Zoe asked in disbelief.

"You're getting treated like this because you don't know how to act otherwise," Ramon responded as he flung her against the counter. "I'm starting to see why your daddy beat y'all's asses; you clearly don't know how to treat a man."

His words cut like a knife and Zoe was unable to contain her rage. She lunged at Ramon and started hitting him as hard as she could and when that didn't seem sufficient, she grabbed a pan off of the stove and wacked him with it. Unfortunately for her, the noise caused Rich to come racing into the kitchen. He grabbed Zoe and held her arms behind her back. "Man, are you going to let her hit you like that? You better put this bitch in her place," he growled at Ramon. And without any further prodding, Ramon backhanded Zoe across the face. "Naw man, you have to hit her where no one can see the bruises," Rich advised. And with his closed fist, Ramon punched Zoe in the ribs as if they were in a professional cage match. Her screams sounded muffled because he literally knocked the wind out of her. Rich let her go and she dropped to the floor like a sack of potatoes. The pain in her mid-section made it difficult to breathe, but in the midst of all her agony, all Zoe could think about was how she would get out of that house.

Ramon knelt down to the floor and whispered, "Now fix me those sandwiches I asked for." Zoe couldn't believe any of what was happening to her. Ramon and Rich left the room and she struggled to her feet. It took every ounce of strength she had to gather the necessary items for their food. She sloppily mad the sandwiches and prayed to God that they would choke to death on them. Zoe carried the plate of food to them and returned to the bedroom. She retrieved her purse and keys and tried to ease out of the back door. But to her dismay, Ramon caught her and ordered her back to their bedroom. Zoe couldn't understand how she'd gotten herself in this position and couldn't stop thinking of how she'd get out of it in one piece.

CHAPTER TWENTY-TWO

Zoe waited patiently for Ramon to leave for work. Her plan was to wait an hour after he left and then leave herself. She figured if she waited an hour it would give him time to double back and see that she was just *relaxing* as he had instructed. Once he was confident that she wasn't trying to leave, he would head on to work and she would run out of that hell hole.

Ramon emerged from the bathroom still in a t-shirt and pajama pants, not his work clothes like Zoe had expected. "Why aren't you dressed for work?" she asked, trying unsuccessfully to hide her disappointment.

"I decided to stay home and nurse you, babe."

"I don't need a nurse, Ramon. All I need is to be left the hell alone." Her tone was venomous.

"You do need me, babe. You need me to love you. I know I messed up, but I love you and all I want now is to take care of you." Zoe looked at him with disgust and then painfully turned over. She couldn't stand to look in his face another second. "Come on; please don't turn your back on me. I can't handle you being this upset with me, Zoe. Don't you know that I need you?"

Zoe turned back over, looked him in the eye and spat, "Well I don't need you! I don't need to be your punching bag, your maid, your cook, or your fucking victim. There is nothing you can ever do for me again except help me pack my things and move."

"Then I guess there's nothing I can do because you're never going to move, you'll never leave me," he said matter-of-factly.

"Watch me!"

"Zoe, baby, don't say that. I'd hate for something to happen to you if you tried to leave. And I know you'd hate for something to happen to your mom or sister if I were to come home and find you and all your stuff gone. Now I've told you that I'm sorry and I really mean it. I never should have allowed Rich to man-handle you like that or call you out of your name. But I swear baby, it'll never happen again."

Ramon's voice was sincere and he gently caressed her as he spoke, but his temporary sincerity meant nothing to Zoe. She and her family had heard it all before. That sorry ass Otis would apologize and bring them all kinds of meaningless gifts every time he sobered up and realized what horrific things he'd done to them. But Ramon was taking it to a new level with his threats against her family. His apology meant nothing to her, but his threats meant everything. Zoe would do whatever she had to; endure just about anything to keep her mom and sister safe.

"Say something babe. I'm pouring my heart out to you and you won't even look at me," Ramon begged.

"Are you serious! What do you want me to say? Do you want me to thank you for threatening my life and the lives of my family? Thank you for slapping me and punching me as if I were some thug on the street? Thank you for using the things I told you about my life, my father, and my abuse against me? You threw that up in my face in a most hurtful way and that showed me what a pathetic man you really are."

"Okay, maybe I deserve that. I realize that none of that was cool and it shouldn't have happened, but you can't stay mad at me forever. Zoe we can have a really good life together, but you'll have to forgive me first."

"Ramon, you are a weak excuse for a human being. I don't know what Rich has on you to make you act like his little bitch, but you need to man up and get him out of your life. As long as he controls you and you are abusive to me, there will be nothing good about either of our lives," Zoe retorted as she tried to get out of bed, but Ramon yanked her back down.

"You call me a bitch again and it'll be the last thing you ever call anyone. Rich doesn't have a damn thing on me. He's my boy, my friend and you will respect him just like you will respect me." He released her arm and allowed her to get up from the bed. "What are you getting ready to do?"

"I'm going to soak in a hot bath, maybe it will help ease my pain."

"I'll do it for you, babe. Relax and I'll run you a hot bubble bath. It'll be ready in just a minute." Ramon jumped up and went into the bathroom to prepare Zoe's bath. Not only did he fill the tub, but he turned on some relaxing Jazz and lit a few scented candles. He returned to the room, undressed Zoe, and helped her ease into the steaming bath. While she relaxed, Ramon went into the kitchen and began to prepare her breakfast.

While Zoe relaxed her body, her mind was flying. She kept imagining different ways that she could get away from Ramon without harm coming to her or her family. And then she wondered if he'd actually try to hurt Martha or Pam if she left him. There was no doubt that he'd beat her senseless, but would he really hurt them? It was a chance that she was not willing to take. She'd been the protector, the planner, the defender of the three of them for so long and now she was the one putting them all in harm's way. Tears began to run down her face as she contemplated having to run from another abuser and uproot her family to yet another city.

Ramon returned to the bathroom, helped Zoe out of the

tub, dried her off and dressed her in fresh pajamas. Then he presented her with a wonderful breakfast of scrambled eggs, bacon, hash browns, toast, and coffee. Zoe was baffled. How could he be so evil one minute and like Prince Charming the next? Was he bipolar, schizophrenic, or just plain crazy? Whatever the case, Zoe knew she had to devise a plan to get away because only God knew what other evil he was capable of.

* * *

April knew that something was terribly wrong with Zoe, but had been unsuccessful in getting her friend to open up to her. Zoe's body showed up at work, but her mind was clearly somewhere else. The glow and joyfulness that was so much a part of her was now gone. Instead, she walked around like a zombie, in a trance that April hadn't been able to shake her out of. After three days of observing this behavior, April called Desi in hopes that he would somehow be able to pull Zoe out of this funk she'd slipped into.

"Desi, I'm really worried about her. She won't talk to me; at lunch she goes and sits in her car and cries. I have no idea what has happened. I don't know how to help her and I'm scared," April confessed.

"I'll be waiting in the parking lot after work and we'll get to the bottom of this, I promise," Desi reassured her.

As promised, when April and Zoe walked out of the credit union, Desi stood in the parking lot right outside of his car. Zoe immediately knew that April had called in the troops. Hard as she'd tried, she hadn't been able to put on a happy face or share with April what had happened at home. She was too embarrassed and ashamed that her life had taken such a drastic and painful turn. The ladies approached Desi and without provocation, Zoe fell into his arms and began to weep. Keeping secrets from April was one thing, but with Desi she wouldn't even try.

He knew her too well and he was her safe haven. He held her tight and whispered, "I'm here, love. Let it out, go ahead and cry. I got you."

Zoe's tears brought tears to April's eyes. Seeing her in such obvious pain was heartbreaking for both April and Desi. And not knowing the source of the pain was maddening. When her sobs started to subside, Desi motioned for April to get in his car as he walked Zoe around to the passenger side. He opened the door, but she didn't get in as he had expected.

"I can't go with you guys," she objected. "I've got to get home, Ramon is expecting me."

"He can wait!" Desi clearly didn't give a damn what Ramon expected. His concern was for Zoe and no one else. "Get in," he instructed and Zoe knew that there was no telling him no. She eased in the car and it wasn't long before they were all sitting in Desi's apartment. He poured them all a glass of wine, looked at Zoe and simply said, "Talk."

"Things with Ramon aren't going the way I'd imagined they would. I wasn't at all ready to move in with him. He's just not the man I thought he was."

"I'll be over this weekend to help you pack and we'll move you right back home with Ms. Martha and Pam," Desi said thinking that it was just that simple.

"I can't," Zoe said. "It's not that easy to walk away from him. He has promised that we'd get counseling and try to work through our issues," she lied. Ramon had made it quite clear that he would never go to another counseling session with her or anyone else. And that lie may have worked except for the fact that she'd already shared with April months ago that there would be no more therapy.

"He's hitting you, isn't he?" The anger in April's voice was unmistakable. "That son-of-a-bitch is putting his hands on you. That's what that scar at your eye was about, wasn't it?" she demanded.

"Yes, that bastard hit me. He punched me, he slapped me, and he threatened me and my family. I hate everything about him, but I can't leave him," Zoe confessed.

Desi jumped up from the couch, went to his bedroom and came back with his Smith and Wesson 9mm gun. He was headed to the door with his keys and gun in hand. No doubt where he was going or what he was going to do. Both Zoe and April jumped from their seats and ran behind him. Zoe grabbed his arm and started pulling him away from the door. "You can't do this, Desi. If it were that simple, I would've killed him myself," she yelled.

"I'm not about to let that coward beat up on you and it is that simple. I'm going to kill that bastard!" Desi exclaimed as he tried to free himself from both the women.

"And then what, go to prison? You can't ruin your life like that Desi. I need you here with me, not locked up in some cell. Please, Desi, don't do this," Zoe pleaded.

"She's right, Desi. This isn't the way to handle things," April added as she held her hand firmly in the center of his chest as if she were strong enough to stop him.

Desi stopped trying to push his way to the door and took a deep breath. "Okay, I'll put the gun back, but I am going to see Ramon. He has got to be dealt with." Desi put the weapon back in his bedroom and once again began his journey to the front door. "Y'all wait here, I'll be back in a little while," he instructed.

"Desi, you can't go confront Ramon. He has vowed to kill me or cause serious harm to Mama and Pam if I try to leave him. He can't know that I have told y'all what's going on, if he does I'll be the one to pay the price," Zoe told them as she took a seat back on the couch. "I am truly between a rock and a hard place. I can't leave and God knows I'm afraid to stay, but I have no choice." Zoe dropped her head in her hands and began to cry again. Her tears angered her because she never viewed herself as a weak, cry baby, but that's just what Ramon was turning her into.

"Look, I have some friends from my old neighborhood that would be happy to put a stop to Ramon. It would be so random that no one would ever be able to connect it back to any of us. All I need is one day and I promise you'll be getting a call from the cops or the hospital saying that there's been an accident." April was stone faced and very serious.

"I swear, I love y'all for wanting to protect me, but I got myself into this mess and I'll have to get myself out of it. Besides, Ramon has safeguards in place. In case something suspicious happens to him, there'll be someone there to take it out on me. He has this friend named Rich and I swear he is like the puppet master. He pulls the strings and Ramon dances. The only reason Ramon punched me the other day was because Rich held my arms and told him to. And just like that ass Otis, Ramon is full of apologies and good deeds after the fact."

"So what are we supposed to do? Sit idly by while you get beat up by this animal," April asked.

"I know it's hard for you both, but I do actually need for you to do nothing. And please, I beg you to keep all of this away from my mom and sister," Zoe responded as she looked in Desi's direction. She knew his first reaction would be to tell Martha what was going on and Zoe couldn't have him doing that. "I'm thinking of possible ways to get out of this situation and I ask y'all to trust me and please be a little patient. I won't let Ramon's bipolar ass kill me or anyone that I love."

"You're asking the impossible Zoe," Desi said. "I can't send you back to him. If something terrible happens to you I would never forgive myself."

"Nothing is going to happen that I can't handle and once I devise a plan, you'll be the first ones to know about it. But for now, please take me back to my car because I've got to get home. I don't want to give him any reason to pick a fight."

"Okay, I'll take you back to your car under one condition," Desi bargained. "Let's stop by the police station and at least file a report. There needs to be some kind of a paper trail."

"Alright, but they better move fast," Zoe agreed.

CHAPTER TWENTY-THREE

Zoe hurried in the house, but only after she'd tucked the police report under the spare tire in her trunk for safe keeping. Luckily, Ramon had decided to meet his friends after work for a beer. She took full advantage of her time alone by packing her valuable jewelry and important papers in a small box and loading them into her car. Although she couldn't leave now, she decided to start getting her vital possessions out of the house little by little.

By the time Ramon returned home, Zoe had eaten, taken a hot bath, and was resting peacefully in bed. The noise that Ramon made when he entered the room woke her, but she didn't move a muscle. She'd hoped that he would be considerate enough to not disturb her and quietly ease into his side of bed and fall fast asleep. Zoe was so thankful when her wish came true. He'd drank so much that he slid out of his clothes and flopped down on the bed like a rag doll and was snoring in no time flat. Zoe laid there thinking about how funny it was that she used to find his snoring funny and cute. Now it was annoying and she prayed that the snoring would cause him to choke to death.

Morning had come so quickly and Zoe had no intention of

laying around wasting the day with Ramon. "Where are you going so early?" Ramon asked as he turned over to see Zoe dressed and ready to leave.

"I promised my mom that I'd take her shopping today and she wants to get an early start."

"Well how long do you plan on being gone?"

"I don't know. I'll just play things by ear and see how the day goes. I know I'll be gone at least long enough to share a dinner out with Mama and Pam."

"I see… Enjoy yourself, don't do anything that would cause any of y'all harm and be back here by 7:00."

"Why do I need to be here by 7:00?" Zoe asked as she slipped her purse on her shoulder and dangled keys in her hand.

"Because I said so and because we're heading over to Rich's place to watch the fight on pay-per-view. Oh and pick up some beer on your way back in. I told Rich that we'd supply the drinks."

Zoe's heart dropped. She knew that an evening at Rich's house would not end well for her. She absolutely hated him and felt sorry for his girlfriend, Candy. Rich was sure to take advantage of every opportunity to make Candy feel like a worthless piece of trash. "Why can't we watch the fight here, just the two of us? I'll pay for it and even pick up dinner," she offered.

"It'll be more fun with friends so do as I've said and be back here on time. If I have to go looking for you, everyone will regret it," Ramon threatened as he got out of bed and moved towards Zoe. He hugged her and kissed her on the forehead. "I love you Zoe, now go have fun."

It seemed that every free moment was spent plotting her escape from Ramon. Zoe drove through the city streets thinking that maybe she could move her mother and sister to another location within the city. Somewhere Ramon would never dream of looking. But then it hit her that he knew where both Martha and Pam worked. Their lives had been so disrupted so many times that Zoe absolutely refused to uproot them again. They would not suffer the loss of their home, jobs, and in Pam's case, love life, all because she screwed around and chose the wrong man. Turning everything over in her brain was giving her a headache, so she decided to forget about it for a while and just enjoy the day with Martha.

"Mama I'm here! Where are you?" Zoe called out.

"I'm in my room baby. Come on back," Martha instructed with a shaky voice.

Zoe walked back to her mother's room and as she crossed the threshold it became evident that something was terribly wrong. Martha was sniffing and wiping tears from her eyes. "Mama, what's wrong, why are you crying?" she asked as she sat on the bed beside Martha. Noticing something in her mother's hands, Zoe reached for it assuming it was the reason for Martha's tears. But she was very reluctant to let it go and when Zoe finally wiggled it from her grip, her jaw dropped. It was a photo shopped picture of Zoe and Pam's naked, mutilated bodies sprawled out on the floor, and the caption read "the only way she'll leave me is over their dead bodies."

"I don't know how he found us, Zoe," Martha sobbed. "I was careful not to tell any family members where we were and I know that Pam was careful as well. I don't know how he found us or how I can protect you girls," she cried with confusion.

Without a name or address attached to the photo, Martha had assumed that it was from Otis. Zoe was the only one he hadn't been able to rape and for that reason she understood how Martha might think it was from him. Otis had always vowed that Zoe was his 'baby girl' and always would be. But Zoe knew better, she knew that the sick creator of the picture was Ramon. He wanted to make sure that she understood how serious he was about her never leaving him. What Zoe didn't understand was why he had to drag her mother into it. Ramon knew what all they had been through; he knew how fragile they were. Zoe had given him no indication that she was leaving so in her mind, this was an unnecessary threat. It was nothing short of evil.

"Mama, has Pam seen this?"

"No, not yet. She spent the night with Alvin and won't be back for another hour or so. When she sees this, she's going to regress right back to that scary, paranoid little girl she was before we moved here."

"No she won't because we're not going to show it to her. There is no reason for her to suffer because of this insanity."

"Zoe, it's only fair that we tell her. She has to know that Otis has found us. This fool could pop up from anywhere and she needs to know to be on the lookout."

"It's not Otis, Mama. Ramon is the one responsible for this picture," Zoe dropped her head and confessed. "I didn't want you to know, it's all so embarrassing, but Ramon is a very dangerous man."

Now it was Zoe's turn to cry and that's just what she did as she recounted some of the incidents of violence that Ramon had inflicted upon her. She told her mother about his threats and how Rich influenced him to take the abuse a little further than what he normally would. Martha held her daughter and they cried together. Martha blamed herself, thinking that if she hadn't subjected Zoe to a violent environment as a child, she wouldn't be in this situation now.

"I'm so sorry, baby; I should have run away from Otis as soon as he showed himself to be violent. If I had you wouldn't be in this situation now. I never should have allowed y'all to witness violence, let alone become the victims of it. This is all my fault and I don't know how to fix it. I don't know how to protect you," Martha sobbed uncontrollably.

"Mama please don't say that. None of this is your fault. Otis was a monster and there was no way you could protect any of us. If you had tried he would've killed you on the spot." Zoe decided that she'd had enough of the tears and grabbed a handful of tissues to wipe her face and blow her nose. "Here Mama, stop crying and clean your face," Zoe demanded. "Pam will be here shortly and she doesn't need to know any of this. I will not allow this to undo all the progress she's made."

"But what are you going to do?" Martha asked as she tried to gain control of her emotions.

"I don't know yet, but one thing I can guarantee you is that I'll figure something out and I won't die in the process. I'm taking my life back, I'm not a piece of property and I don't belong to Ramon. It may take me a minute, but I will get out of this situation and live the life that I deserve."

Zoe took the disturbing picture and hid it in her car. She retrieved the box of her jewelry and papers and took them up to the apartment. She tucked them in the back of her mother's closet for safe keeping. By the time Pam arrived home, Martha and Zoe had managed to pull themselves together and act like they were just sitting around waiting for Pam to show up so that the shopping could commence. But when Pam entered the house, she looked as if she'd seen a ghost. Her skin was pale and tears were streaming down her face.

"Pam what's wrong?" Zoe asked even though she was afraid to hear the answer.

"I just saw Otis."

"Where, where did you see him?" Zoe screamed.

"Outside, he was standing between two cars right out front," Pam sniffled.

Martha went to comfort her child and Zoe ran out the door to see if she could spot her father. Not only was Otis nowhere to be found, but Zoe didn't even spot two cars that were parked directly beside one another. She ran to the back side of the building and still nothing. Zoe ran back up the stairs and into the apartment. "I didn't see him anywhere. Are you sure it was Otis?"

"I could have sworn it was but maybe I was wrong," Pam said as she shook her head.

"While you were out looking for him, I called up his sister. She said that Otis hasn't left Washington since being released. As a matter of fact, she just saw him yesterday," Martha informed them.

"I feel so stupid," Pam said. "But I could have sworn that was him, I mean it looked just like him. A few years older and not as heavy, but still it looked just like him."

* * *

Zoe was running a little late but still made time to stop by the police station and have the disturbing photo of she and Pam added to her file. She wanted to provide the cops with every bit of incriminating information that she could so that if anything happened to her or Pam, they would know who was responsible. She hustled in the front door and was greeted by an agitated Ramon.

"Where have you been? I told you to be on time and here you are twenty minutes late. Where were you?" Ramon barked.

"Babe, I'm so sorry I'm running behind. I was late dropping Mama and Pam off."

"You got five minutes to get yourself together. If you're not ready when I head out that door, that's your ass, you understand?"

"I'll only be a minute," Zoe reassured him. She darted off to the bedroom, ripped off her clothes and jumped into the other outfit she'd laid out earlier. She quickly stepped into a pair of flats, smeared on some lipstick and walked back into the front room. "I'm ready."

"What's with the little flat shoes? Go throw on a pair of those sexy heels I like to see you in."

"We're just going to Rich's house and I want to be comfortable. It's a fight party for goodness sake, not a debutant ball," Zoe said sarcastically. But one look into his eyes let her know that her desire to wear comfortable shoes wouldn't be worth the fight. She slipped on her black pumps and they headed out for the evening.

Candy opened the door with a big smile plastered on her face, but Zoe couldn't tell if it was genuine or not. It was hard to read Candy, she had a great body and pretty face, but her eyes looked so tired, so hopeless. "Y'all come on in," she said as she waved them in with her hand. "Make yourselves comfortable and let's get ready to enjoy the fight."

"Hey Candy, you've got it smelling good in here," Ramon complimented.

"Hi Candy, it's good to see you," Zoe smiled. "It is smelling good in here. Is there anything I can help you with in the kitchen?"

"I've just about got everything done, but you can come on in there with me for a little girl talk while the guys do their thing," Candy offered.

As they passed through the living room, Zoe waved hello to Rich and attempted to give him a smile but her expression looked more like she'd just encountered a foul smell. Zoe had never been any good at hiding her feelings, they were usually written all over her face, and her hatred for Rich for no exception.

"Looking good Zoe. I'm digging those heels," Rich said with a smile.

"Thanks," Zoe replied dryly without even looking in his direction. She just continued her short journey to the kitchen

Rich chuckled, "Your girl is a trip with her little snooty ass. She don't even know how to say thank you without an attitude."

"Nah man, she's all good. Probably just acting that way because I was rushing her. I swear she's slow as hell," Ramon commented, not wanting Rich to know how Zoe really felt about him.

"Well attitude or not, she is still fine as hell. I bet you be wearing that ass out, don't you?"

Ramon blushed like a little school boy as he slapped Rich's hand. "Man you know how it is, I gotta make it do what it do," he boasted.

While the guys talked their trash, Zoe decided to engage Candy in a little more conversation. She wanted to know if Candy's life with Rich was as bad as hers was with Ramon. "So tell me Candy, how long have you and Rich been dating?"

"Oh Lord, it seems like forever, but in actuality we've been together for about four and a half years. Can you believe we met in a strip club?" Candy asked as she chuckled and shook her head.

"Really? Were you a dancer or were you just hanging out there with your girls?" Zoe asked. In this day and time it seemed like women hung out at strip clubs just like the men did and she didn't want to make any incorrect assumptions.

"I was hanging out with a large group of friends celebrating. A co-worker was getting married and we thought we'd throw him a surprise co-ed bachelor party. We were having a ball until Rich mistook me for a stripper. I never understood why, I wasn't looking trashy or anything and his little mistake almost caused a brawl between him and the guys that were in our group. But he apologized, said he didn't want any beef and bought my entire party a round of drinks. Stupid me, I thought he was a baller and when he managed to catch me alone he apologized again, offered to buy me dinner, and the rest is history."

"Can I ask you one more question?"

"Zoe, you can ask me anything you like," Candy reassured.

"Whenever I see you you're always smiling but still look so sad. Why is that, aren't you happy with Rich?"

"Damn, what's a man gotta do to get some food up in here? Y'all need to hurry your asses up, we're hungry," Rich bellowed from the other room.

"I'm sad for the same reasons you are Zoe," she admitted as she finished placing food on a tray. "We'll be out in just a second," she yelled back to Rich.

"Have you ever thought about leaving," Zoe's curiosity propelled her to ask.

"Sure, I packed my things one day and by the time Rich got

home from work I was long gone. But he found me at my cousin's house, did this to me, and threatened to kill my mama if I didn't come back," Candy said as she raised her skirt to reveal a six inch jagged scar that had been etched into her thigh. "We'd better get this food out to them before they get ugly."

Zoe spent the rest of the evening watching Candy pretend to be happy. And although she didn't know when or how, she knew that she had to get away from Ramon. She couldn't imagine spending the rest of her life under this suffocating cloud of misery. Somehow, some way, she would have to escape or die trying.

CHAPTER TWENTY-FOUR

Alvin had been such a comfort to Pam and to Martha for that matter. They had not bothered to tell Zoe that Pam had seen who she thought was Otis another three times. Of course the first thing Pam wanted to do was pick up the phone and have Zoe run right over. But Martha knew all that Zoe was dealing with and didn't want to add any additional stress on top of what was already weighing her down. Besides, Martha was convinced that Pam was just imagining it all.

After the second sighting, it took Martha a solid hour to calm Pam down. The girl was all but hysterical and Martha had to restrain herself from slapping the hell out of her just to shut her up. But instead, she got on the phone with Alvin and he immediately raced over. He did a thorough search of the surrounding apartment buildings but came up empty handed. And it was the same thing each time, Pam saw Otis, but no one else did. Concerned for her mental state, Alvin decided to escort Pam to an emergency therapy session.

As comfortable as Pam had always been with her therapist, Dr. Shellie Frost, she was feeling incredibly uncomfortable about having to pay her a visit under these circumstances. Her mom or Alvin had never told her that they thought she was having hallucinations, but she knew that's what they were thinking. She would be crushed if that's what the therapist thought as well. She and Alvin had been waiting patiently in the waiting room and with loving eyes, Alvin watched as Pam nervously picked at her cuticles. He was worried that if she kept trying to pluck away dry skin her hands would begin to bleed.

"Sweetheart, why don't you give those poor hands a break?" he spoke softly as he took her hand in his.

"I'm sorry, you must think I'm losing my mind," Pam replied, fearful that he really did think she was going crazy. Alvin had been the best thing to ever happen to Pam and she didn't want this, whatever it was, to make him want to leave her. Pam's eyes began to water at the thought of separating from her love and she was grateful that the receptionist called her name before a tear could fall. They were ushered into the office where Shellie was waiting.

"Good afternoon, come on in and take a seat," Shellie offered in a cheerful voice.

"Hi, Shellie, thank you for seeing us on such short notice." Pam took a seat on the couch and Alvin sat right beside her, still holding her hand.

"No problem, I'll always make time for my favorite patient. Now tell me what's going on."

"The other weekend I could have sworn that I saw my father. I mean I would have bet my life that it was him but no one else saw him. And since then I've seen him three more times," Pam's voice trembled.

"The last couple of times that you thought you saw him, did you attempt to speak to him, call his name, or anything?"

"No, I mean I called his name the first time and he just stood there and looked at me, but these last few times I…I… wasn't quite as positive it was him so I just hurried away," Pam stuttered.

"What makes you so positive that it was really him the first time?" Shellie asked softly.

"His face, the way he was standing, watching me, it was eerie. Every muscle in my body tensed up and I know it might sound crazy, but I know my father and I'll go to my grave believing that it was Otis."

"I see..." Shellie said as she tapped her pen on the arm of her chair. "Alvin, have you been with her any of the other times she thought she saw him?"

"Unfortunately not. Either she was on her way to meet me or we'd just separated. But I tell you, I hate what this is doing to her," he replied with concern etched in his face.

"Well what's important is that you're here for her and continue to support her during all of this. And Pam, I don't know if you really saw Otis or not that first time, but I think the shock of that encounter has triggered a serious case of paranoia. I think that you realize that the other sightings really weren't of your father, but you're so afraid of the possibility of seeing him that you're now imagining that he's everywhere. Does that sound like it could be what's going on with you?"

"I suppose so," Pam spoke softly. Tears started to run down her face. "I know I saw him that first time and I'm not crazy, Shellie. I'm not some paranoid schizophrenic," she wept.

"Oh Pam, I know that! I simply mean that the shock of that first encounter has you so terribly afraid that you're now worried about seeing Otis everywhere you go. Now please tell me if I have it wrong?"

"That sounds right, Shellie," Pam confessed. "So what's next, do you want to institutionalize me or put me on some meds that's going to have me walking around like a zombie?"

"Surely you don't want to do either of those things," Alvin chimed in. "She's not some nut case."

"No, guys, I actually don't plan to do anything except schedule more visits with you. I want us to be able to talk more frequently and work through this without taking any drastic measures. Besides, you're doing great on your job, you're in a loving relationship, and your family life is good. We don't want to jeopardize any of that or take the joy out of your life. We simply need to manage the anxiety of this Otis business and we'll do that through good old fashioned conversation and techniques to help you determine if you're really seeing Otis or just another Joe on the street."

Pam was relieved that Shellie hadn't wanted to take any drastic measures and relieved more so that Alvin had been and vowed to continue to be by her side, to support her through all of this non sense. They had left the therapist's office and grabbed some lunch at the Flying Biscuit. Alvin absolutely loved that place, especially their famous creamy grits and the scrambled eggs with collard greens and onions. Pam thought that the restaurant was decent and always had the same chocolate chip muffin and cappuccino. She preferred to eat elsewhere, but her man loved it so she happily tolerated it. With full bellies, they made their way back to Pam and Martha's apartment. Martha was still at work for at least another four hours so the love birds decided to chill there and take a little nap.

They hadn't been laying down a good five minutes before thoughts of a nap were replaced by thoughts of making love. Alvin touched Pam's body gently, just the way she liked. He was always mindful of how delicate he needed to be with her. It was his goal to replace every fear Pam had of men and of love making with a beautiful memory. He kissed her sweetly and whispered how much he loved her as he freed her from her clothes. Softly he nibbled at her neck and her breasts and traveled south to kiss and lick her pleasure spot. Pam moaned her approval and when she thought she could take no more, he whispered, "Are you ready baby?"

"Ummm yes..." Pam purred seductively.

Alvin entered her with care and allowed her to set the pace of their strokes. And gradually they went from slow and methodical to free and rhythmic. There were no acrobatics, no changing positions like porn stars, no dirty talk, but for them it was absolutely beautiful.

Pam and Alvin fell asleep and stayed that way until Martha came home, walked through the house and found them on the bed butt naked. "Oh my Lord! Pamela get your naked tail up and put on some clothes," Martha exclaimed as she turned and stumbled out of the room. "Damn it, I stubbed my toe," she cried out still trying to make her way to the front of the apartment.

Pam and Alvin had jumped up scrambling for clothes when they realized what was going on. "Mama, I'm so sorry," Pam shouted from her room as she jumped up and down trying to get her pants on. "I can't believe we fell asleep like this!"

"I can, that's what happens when you have good sex," Alvin teased as he pulled on his shirt.

"This is no time to joke," Pam scolded with a crooked little grin on her face. "Now hurry up and finish dressing and come up front ready to apologize."

"Yes ma'am. I'll be up in a minute," Alvin said sheepishly as he playfully smacked her on the butt.

Timidly, Pam walked to the living room and peeked to see what Martha was doing. She wasn't able to tell if the scowl on her mother's face was from the pain of stubbing her toe or the disgust of finding her and Alvin the way she had. Either way, she was ready to grovel and beg for forgiveness. "Mama, I am so sorry for what you saw. I never wanted you to know that me and Alvin were doing that sort of thing and I certainly didn't want you to find out like this. But if it's any conciliation, we truly love each other. Mama, please forgive me, I'm so sorry."

"Child I know what you and Alvin been doing for months. I mean really, Pam, you stay at his house at least twice a week and I certainly didn't think y'all were playing Go Fish all night. You're a grown woman and I could care less about your sex life. I just don't want to have y'all's naked behinds tooted up in my face. I mean at least have the decency to close and lock your door," Martha huffed.

"Hi Ms. Martha," Alvin whispered as he hid behind the

corner of the wall. "I'm sorry you saw my junk and I know it makes you want me, Ms. Martha, but I belong to Pam."

"Boy, don't nobody want your bony behind." Martha couldn't help but smile. Alvin was such a sweet and silly guy, it was impossible to stay upset with him. "Just make sure I don't see the crack of your ass again."

Alvin walked on into the room and gave Martha a serious apology, vowing to never let anything that disrespectful happen again. Within a few minutes they were all chuckling about the embarrassing situation. But it wasn't long before the conversation turned to Pam and Alvin's earlier therapy session. They filled Martha in on everything that Shellie said and she was more relieved than she was willing to admit that Pam wasn't completely off her rocker. It wasn't that Martha thought her daughter had completely lost it, but she found a great deal of comfort in knowing that the therapist didn't feel that Pam was teetering on the brink of insanity.

CHAPTER TWENTY-FIVE

Everything seemed to provoke an argument lately and as the work day came to an end, Zoe cringed at the thought of going home. She knew that Ramon would find something else to fight about. It didn't matter how minuscule it might be, he was full swing into his fighting season and anything would set him off. She'd gone to visit her mom and sister the other day and had forgotten to run the dishwasher before leaving. When she returned home, every drinking glass they had was broken on the kitchen floor. He told her that since she was too stupid to wash the dishes she didn't deserve to have them. Then he flung her to the floor where shards of glass cut her hand and ankle. He wouldn't let her up to tend to her wounds until all the glass and blood had been cleaned up.

April knew of some of the issues between Zoe and Ramon, but wasn't fully aware of how much things had escalated. She didn't know how Ramon now made her perform for him on the regular basis. He'd taken the playful gesture of her being his private dancer to a demeaning and degrading level. He'd make her put on ridiculous stripper outfits and treat her like a trick in a club. April often asked her if things had gotten worse, if Ramon was more abusive, but Zoe simply said no. Embarrassment and fear kept her from confessing the severity of her situation to anyone. The constant threats against her family were enough for Ramon to keep her in check. But his threats of mutilating her or burning her with acid further cemented her place as his girlfriend, servant, punching bag, or whatever else he wanted her to be.

"Zoe, someone is on line three for you," one of the other bank employees called out.

"Thank you," she nodded as she picked up the receiver. "This is Zoe Shaw. How may I help you?"

"You can give me some money bank lady."

"Desi you are so silly," Zoe laughed. "How are you today, my love?"

"I'm fine, but the question is how: are you? We haven't had a good sit down conversation in a while."

"I know and I'm sorry for that. I've been so caught up in my own stuff lately that I've neglected you."

"Oh no sweetie, I'm fine. I want to talk because I'm worried about you. I'm cooking a great dinner today. Why don't you swing by after work for some good food and conversation?"

"You're cooking?" Zoe asked knowing that he wasn't.

"You know, I'm cooking, I'm getting take out…same thing," he teased. "The point is I want you to stop by for a while. Please with sugar on top?" he begged.

"Okay, but just for a little bit. And you have to promise not to get mad when it's time for me to leave. I've already said I can only stay for a little bit, got it?"

"Got it… I'll see you a little later and you can bring April if you like."

"No, I think I'd just like to spend time with you. It's been a while since we had a moment to ourselves." She had grown to love April, but she was still too embarrassed to let her know how bad things had gotten. But Desi, she'd tell him any and everything without hesitation or embarrassment.

"Cool babe, it's your call. I'll see you later and I love you."

"Love you too. Bye."

"Who do you love?" April asked as she walked up behind Zoe as she hung up the phone. Zoe jumped and turned around like she was afraid for her life. "And why so jumpy?"

"Girl I didn't know you were behind me," Zoe chuckled as she grabbed her chest. "You know I'm getting old and the ticker can't take any surprises."

"Umm hmm..." April grunted as she wondered why her friend was really so on edge. "Was that a new man you met or something? Someone that no one is supposed to know about?"

"Child please, that was Desi calling to say hello."

"Oh, I was getting excited at the possibility of there being some sexy mystery man who was trying to steal you away from Ramon."

"Humph, you read too many romance novels girl. This is the real world and sexy mystery men don't exist in it," Zoe remarked.

"When did you become so cynical?"

"I'm not cynical, just realistic." Zoe thought about how she'd first viewed Ramon as a sexy mystery man and had fallen for him hook, line, and sinker. But once she'd fallen, he reverted back to the abusive cave man that she'd always known men to be. So as far as she was concerned, there were no good men, no knights in shining armor, no heroes, just monsters.

"One day someone is going to come along and prove you wrong," April said as she lovingly squeezed her friends hand and walked away.

Desi opened the door and greeted Zoe with a big hug and kiss. "Come on in, beautiful." He escorted her to the family room where she plopped down on the big oversized sofa. "Here you go doll. I made this just before you rang the doorbell," he said as he handed over a wine goblet filled with Zoe's favorite merlot.

"Thank you Desi. How did you know I'd need this?"

"I could hear the stress in your voice earlier and figured you could use a tasty drink. Now do you want to go ahead and eat or sit here and chat for a while?"

"Let's sit here for a while. This sofa, hell the whole place is so beautiful yet so comfortable. Can I move in," Zoe teased.

"You know we have an extra bedroom and it's yours if you want it," Desi offered seriously. He would gladly move her in, support her, and do anything else it would take to get and keep her away from that damn Ramon.

"You're the sweetest... So tell me, how are things between you and Kirk? Have y'all decided when you're flying out to get married?"

"The whole marriage thing has been put on hold for a bit but we're still doing great. Kirk seems to have let go of all that jealousy crap and is trusting in our relationship more. I've been better about keeping more business appropriate hours and letting him know in advance about any late meetings. Seems that a little consideration goes a long way. But enough about us, how are you doing?"

Zoe took a big gulp of wine, looked up at Desi, and burst into tears. She sobbed as she told him of everything she'd been enduring. She confessed about the broken glasses, about the ice cold showers when she didn't perform to his sexual satisfaction, how he'd choke her whenever she spoke to him with disrespect, and the nights he'd literally kick her out of bed and make her sleep on the floor if she refused him sex. She held nothing back, not even the fact that Ramon had made her eat off the floor when he said that the meal she cooked wasn't fit for a dog. She was embarrassed yet relieved to be able to tell someone of her own personal hell.

Desi held her and cried with her. His heart broke for Zoe, but he was also so angry that it was all he could do to keep from jumping up, grabbing his gun, and going after that son-of-a-bitch Ramon. "You can't go back there Zoe. You can't sit around and wait for that sick fucker to kill you."

"He has made it clear that if I try to leave not only will he hurt me, but Pam and Mama will suffer as well. And he doesn't just say that he'll kill them or have them killed, it's how he says they will suffer before death comes for them. I can't take that chance, I can't risk their lives," Zoe cried.

"Do they know what you're going through over there? Because I know that they would gladly take their chances if they knew all of this."

"Mama knows some of what's going on, but not everything. Pam knows nothing, she would be too freaked out and wouldn't be able to handle it and the supposed Otis sighting. Hell, she's already in therapy, if she knew about the threats against her life they'd have to commit her ass."

"Well if it's going to get you away from Ramon, let them commit her and then you and Martha can go into hiding until we can come up with a more permanent plan."

"You know I can't do that to Pam."

"But we've got to do something, Zoe."

"Yes we do and let's start by refilling my glass," she said with a half-smile as she wiped away her tears. "My visit here today wasn't to try to come up with a solution, but to just have a good cry, share a good meal, and relax for a bit. So now that I've purged, can I please have some more wine and some food?"

Desi reluctantly agreed to drop their current conversation and move on with dinner and drinks. He'd had Zoe's favorite Chinese restaurant deliver their meal and he popped the cork on another bottle of wine. As they ate and drank the mood changed, it became lighter. They laughed as they reminisced about old times and some of the kids they grew up with. Desi had learned to embrace his past and forgive his high school tormentors. Now the ones that tortured him were either strung out on drugs, in prison, or just plain ole miserable. Although both of them had serious challenges growing up, they still had plenty to laugh about and reminisce on because they'd always had each other.

Three hours later, the friends lay on the sofa full of food and wine and were sleeping like babies. They were oblivious to the fact that Ramon had just left Martha's place looking for Zoe, but when no one answered the door, he decided that Desi's house would be his next stop. The intense banging on the door jolted Desi and Zoe from their slumber. Annoyed, Desi went and yanked the front door open to see who had the nerve to approach his home like that. When he saw Ramon, he slammed the door in his face, but Ramon flung it right back open.

"Where is she?" he demanded. But as soon as he turned his head, he saw Zoe scrambling to get her shoes on. "What the hell are you doing over here so late? You were supposed to be home hours ago."

"I'm sorry, I just stopped by to chat for a while and"

"You don't have to explain yourself to him," Desi spat as he cut her off mid-sentence. "You're a grown ass woman who can come and go as you please."

"Mind your own damn business bro. This ain't got nothing to do with you."

"Zoe is my business and when you banged on my door like you were damn SWAT you made it even more my business. And now that you know she's safe and sound you can step. She'll be home when she gets home."

"She's coming home now. Zoe get your stuff and let's go. Now!" he yelled when she didn't immediately move.

Zoe jumped up, grabbed her purse and keys, and walked towards Ramon. He grabbed her arm forcefully and when he did Desi stepped in and pushed him back. "Man, don't be yanking her like that. This is a female and she's not to be man-handled."

"Bro, I told you that this wasn't your business, now sit your punk ass down," Ramon barked as he slammed Desi into a table causing him to fall.

"I got your punk!" Desi jumped to his feet and before Ramon could react, Desi sucker punched him in the face, busting his lip and knocking him to the ground. As Ramon tried to scramble to his feet, Desi ran and retrieved his hand gun.

When Ramon looked up, he was looking down the barrel of a Smith and Wesson. "Who's the punk now, huh? Don't you know I'll blow your fucking head off?"

"Desi no, please put the gun down," Zoe begged. "He's not worth it Desi, he's not worth your freedom. I need you and you can't be of any help to me if you're in prison. Please don't shoot." Zoe stepped in front of Ramon as she continued to talk. "We're just gonna leave Desi. I love you and I'll call you later, okay? Just put the gun down." She grabbed the doorknob as she and Ramon backed out and gently closed the door on the way. Once they were outside, she took off down the stairs and ran to her car. Ramon was hot on her heels but didn't catch her before she slammed the car door.

Ramon stared at Zoe through the car window and motioned for her to roll it down. She cracked the window, but Ramon didn't make any sudden moves because he was aware that Desi stood only feet away still holding his weapon. "Go straight home. I'll follow you and if at any time you go in a different direction, I'll head to Ms. Martha's house and spend a little quality time with her. You understand?" Zoe nodded her head, rolled up the window, and waited for Ramon to start his car and pull up behind hers.

CHAPTER TWENTY-SIX

Zoe trembled with fear so badly that she couldn't even put the key in the lock. Ramon placed his hand over hers and she jumped, but surprisingly he gently used her hand to guide the key into the lock and open the door. They walked in the house and when the door closed behind them Zoe braced herself for the hit that she knew was coming. But there was no hit, no slap, no kick, just the holding of her hand as he guided her back to the bedroom. "Why don't you take a hot shower and then put on that red outfit I like with some heels. I'll be waiting for you in the den, but no rush, I'm just going to relax for a few." Ramon paused at the mirror and cleaned the dried blood from the corner of his mouth before leaving the room and closing the door.

The hot water pouring over Zoe's body was incredibly soothing. She slowly lathered her body and let the lavender scent of her body wash relax her nerves. And while some of her tension was eased, she was still concerned with what Ramon had in store for her. She couldn't make herself believe that all he wanted was for her to dance in some sexy lingerie and all would be forgotten. He had to have something else up his sleeve. Zoe finished her shower, dried and lotioned her body. She took a look in the full length mirror once she was dressed in red bra, thong, garter belt, thigh high stockings and six inch heels. She remembered how proud she used to be of her incredible body, but now she just viewed it as a source for her own punishment.

Zoe took a deep breath and walked out of the bedroom, but as she turned the corner to the small den she let out a loud squeal and ran back towards the room. She was mortified to see Rich and Harvey sitting in there with Ramon. "Zoe, get your ass back out here," Ramon barked.

"Okay, give me a second to cover up."

"No, I want you out here like you are. I want you out here dancing now!"

Zoe went back to the bedroom, slammed the door, and locked it. She started grabbing clothes and trying to hurry and dress. But before she could get one pant leg on, Ramon knocked the door off the hinges. "I swear if you don't get your ass out there now I will kill you. You will dance and act like you like it, do you understand?"

"No," Zoe sobbed. "I can't go out there and dance for them. I'm not taking my clothes off for them, Ramon. Please, please don't make me do this," she pleaded in between sobs.

But all of her begging was in vain. Ramon grabbed her by the throat and began to squeeze. "Unless you're ready to die up in here you'll get your ass out there and dance." He released her neck only to yank her by the arm, drag her out of the room and up the hall and fling her to the floor. "Rich, hit that button for the music," Ramon instructed. He then walked over to Zoe and kicked her in the leg. "Get your ass up and dance."

"Man, stop treating your girl like that. Don't embarrass her like this," Harvey spoke up, but Rich immediately shut him down.

"Harvey, sit back, shut up, and let this man handle his business and his bitch," Rich instructed.

Harvey shook his head in disgust and watched as Ramon kicked Zoe once more as she cried. He wasn't sure if she cried more because of the pain or the humiliation. His heart hurt for her, but he knew there were serious limits on how much he could come to her defense without having to go blow-for-blow with Rich. As Zoe slowly stood to her feet, Harvey imagined how angry he would be if some fool tried to treat his sister this way. He couldn't understand how Ramon felt it was okay to treat a good woman like Zoe with such disrespect. It's not like she was some whore off the street, she was a beautiful, smart, successful, sexy woman that deserved to be treated like a queen. And as gorgeous as she was, as perfect as her body was, Harvey diverted his eyes from her. He didn't want her to feel yet another pair of lustful eyes on her.

"I don't have all night Zoe, dance or I'll find a way to make you and I promise you won't like it," Ramon warned.

Zoe listened to the hard-core rap music, the vulgarity and sexually explicit lyrics seemed to fuel Ramon's vicious fire. But she desperately wanted to avoid the painful consequences of not following his instructions, so slowly she began to sway to the music.

"You've gotta do better than that," Ramon barked. "Dance like you dance when it's just us." Reluctantly she moved her body with a little more enthusiasm. She rolled her hips, dropped low, and tossed her hair, but she never stopped sobbing, her tears never ceased to fall. "Yeah baby, that's it," Ramon encouraged.

"Ramon, you are one lucky man," Rich acknowledged. "She is fine as hell. If I were you I'd be tearing that up every night." Rich was damn near salivating over Zoe.

Rich's words made Zoe nauseous. Her stomach turned and it was all she could do to keep from throwing up. Then she heard Ramon say, "And she gives the best head," and sickness was replaced by disgust. Her hatred for him grew every single time he opened his mouth.

"I've danced for you, may I please go put my clothes on," Zoe pleaded.

"Let's ask the fellas," Ramon suggested. "Y'all satisfied or you wanna see more?"

"I don't need to see anymore," Harvey replied. He looked up at Zoe, she returned his glance and mouthed thank you. He nodded and again diverted his eyes.

"Shit man, you've got me fantasizing about that good head. Since I can't have that let me at least have one more dance," Rich's requested with a dirty look in his eyes.

"I don't know man; my girl here likes to lay up with other men so she may like helping you out with that fantasy. Ain't that right, Zoe?"

Fear gripped Zoe and panic set in. "I don't know what you mean. I've never laid up with another man and I'm not making anyone's fantasy come true," she said as her voice trembled and fresh tears burned her eyes.

"You were laid up with that punk, Desi. Shoes off and stretched out on the sofa, wrapped in his arms, am I right? Every time I turn around you're laid up with that bastard!"

"You know he's gay and more importantly, he's like my brother, we're best friends," Zoe explained.

"Well tonight we're going to pretend that my boy Rich is like your new best friend. Now help your new friend out with that fantasy of his," Ramon ordered.

"Oh hell, this is my lucky night!" Rich exclaimed as he started to unbuckle his pants.

Zoe turned and tried to run from the room, but Ramon caught her by the hair and pulled her back. "I know you've done this shit for that damn Desi, so just pretend like this is his punk ass." He then forced her to her knees and told Rich to come and get it as he continued to hold a fist full of her hair. Rich jumped to his feet and Harvey looked on in shock. He couldn't believe what he was seeing. But as Rich approached Zoe with his shaft in hand, Harvey snapped out of his trance and jumped up.

"Enough of this shit," Harvey yelled. "Let her go, let her go now," he ordered.

"You don't have to get mad man, she can do you too," Ramon laughed.

"I don't want her to do shit for me and she's not going to do anything for y'all either. Now let her up," he shouted as he shoved Ramon back, making him lose his grip on her hair. "Get up Zoe, go get dressed and go now!"

"What the hell's wrong with you Harvey? You ain't running nothing up in here," Ramon shouted as he came at Harvey with clinched fists. He took a swing, but Harvey ducked, came back up and clocked Ramon square in the face knocking him off his feet. And while Ramon tried to recover, Rich hastily dressed and took steps towards Harvey, but Harvey didn't back up or back down, he stood his ground ready to knock the hell out of Rich as well. But that wouldn't happen because the truth was that Rich was a weak ass that couldn't handle a fight with a man. He limited his abuse to women, those he knew he could over power.

Zoe emerged from the back fully dressed with her purse and car keys in hand. Ramon tried to grab her, but she managed to dodge his grasp. She ran out the door and Harvey stood guard while she made her get away. But what she didn't realize was that after she left, her defender was jumped by both Ramon and Rich and severely beaten. Harvey was thrown out in the street with two black eyes, cracked ribs, a fractured clavicle, and multiple bruises and lacerations. But he never regretted stepping in to save Zoe.

CHAPTER TWENTY-SEVEN

Desi swung his car into the parking space right beside Zoe's car. He jumped out and starting jogging towards Martha's apartment. As he began his ascension up the stairs, he noticed two men standing nearby and one of them had a strong resemblance to Otis. But common sense told Desi that if Otis were in town, he certainly wouldn't be hanging out, smoking cigarettes, and shooting the breeze outside of Martha's home. He continued his journey and knocked on the door. "It's Desi y'all, come on and open the door."

Pam swung the door open and as Desi looked past her, he saw Zoe looking disheveled with her eyes swollen from crying. He walked in, fell to his knees right in front of Zoe and wrapped her in his arms. She had called him from the car as she was making her escape from Ramon's. She was crying hysterically and could only manage to tell him that she was headed to her mom's house. When she first got to Martha's, she walked in on her mom, sister, and Alvin laughing at one of Tyler Perry's movies and the antics of Madea. They all heard the door close, looked up, and saw Zoe. Martha didn't even know what had happened, but knew that her daughter had just gone through hell. She held her baby and cried with her.

With everyone gathered around her, Zoe began to recount the events of the evening. And despite her concern for Pam, she shared every sordid detail. Her mother and sister wept like babies while both Desi and Alvin became more infuriated with each word she spoke. Alvin had become a part of the family and felt it was now his appointed duty to protect not only Pam, but Martha and Zoe as well. Pam cried and through sobs demanded that they call the police. But with only a couple of bruises, Zoe thought it would be pointless. Once Zoe finished with the sick details, Desi jumped to his feet and headed to the door with Alvin hot on his heels. Neither of the men spoke, but the anger that consumed them and distorted their faces said all that needed to be said.

"No, no, please guys don't go over there. Don't do anything stupid," Zoe pleaded. "You both have too much to lose to be over there trying to fight or get revenge. Please just sit back down," she cried as she pulled Desi by the arm.

"Do you seriously think that we're going to let that son-of-a-bitch treat you like that? Hell no, he's going to pay for this!" Alvin exclaimed and everyone was surprised. He was always so mild mannered and relaxed, this was a side of Alvin that they'd never seen.

Desi yanked his arm back. "He's right, they treated you like trash. That bastard kicked you like you were some stray dog. Alvin's right, he needs to be handled, taught a lesson, and that bastard gone learn tonight.

"No, please, please don't go," Zoe cried as they slammed the door on their way out.

"Mama why didn't y'all try and help me stop them?"

"They know what they're doing and that sorry excuse for a man Ramon needs to know that he can't get away with abusing you. We need to sit back and let the men handle this one," Martha said matter-of-factly.

"I couldn't agree more," Pam added.

"I'm sorry, I don't agree. The only thing that can come out of their altercation is Desi and Alvin either being hurt, arrested, or both," Zoe proclaimed.

As Desi and Alvin turned onto Ramon's street, they were surprised to see an ambulance and police lights flashing brightly. There had to be at least four cop cars and it appeared that the EMS workers were tending to a patient in the back of the ambulance. Desi pulled the car to the side of the road and they both jumped out to go see what was going on. As they got closer to the commotion, they could see the cops escorting a handcuffed Ramon and Rich out of the house. Unable to contain his anger, Desi took off running in their direction with the intention of beating all hell out of Ramon. But before he could reach his target, Alvin grabbed him by the arm, "Chill out man. We're not trying to get locked up too," he warned. The two of them approached the cops and demanded that charges be pressed against Ramon on behalf of Zoe.

"Officer, these bastards attacked our friend tonight. They kicked her and tried to sexually assault her," Alvin said sternly.

"Well your friend will have to come down to the station and file a report. Her statement coupled with that of the other victim could keep these two locked up for a while," the officer advised.

As Ramon was ushered past them, he gave Desi a dirty look and then spat in his face. Desi reacted swiftly with a fist to Ramon's face. "Hey, step back," another officer warned Desi. Thankfully, there was no mention of Desi being arrested and he had the satisfaction of watching the blood gush from Ramon's nose.

"Save your spit for your bunk mate you little bitch," Desi said venomously.

"Step back and shut up or you'll be going down with him," the officer offered one last warning.

Before Desi could say another word, Alvin grabbed him by the shoulder and pulled him away. "Dude, chill out... Let's go see who's in the ambulance. I've got a feeling it's the guy that came to Zoe's defense." The EMS workers were stabilizing the gurney in preparation for the short ride to the county hospital. Alvin peeked inside and saw a badly beaten young man moaning in pain. "Are you Harvey?" Alvin shouted into the ambulance.

"Yeah, who's asking?" Harvey asked in between moans.

"We're friends of Zoe. We just wanted to say thank you man." Alvin barely got the words out before the EMS worker shut the door. "Come on Desi. Let's go over here and see if these women will tell us what happened. Let's see if they know about what they did to Zoe." The two men approached the small group and eavesdropped for a moment, but when the whispers got too low to hear, Alvin thought 'screw it' and decided to simply start asking questions. "Excuse me ladies, I don't mean to bother y'all, but what happened here tonight?"

The women all looked at each other for a moment as if to ask "who the hell are you?" but then the short, stout, blond woman decided to be the mouthpiece of the group. "My daughter over there," she said pointing to the young lady talking with cops. "She came running in the house screaming for me to call the cops. She said someone had been hit. She ran back out and talked to the man until the ambulance got here. Turns out the poor guy hadn't been hit, but had been beaten up real bad."

"Did you hear anything before your daughter came running in?" Desi quizzed.

"I mean I heard some yelling coming from over there, but I didn't really think anything about it. It's not like yelling and screaming is uncommon for that house," the woman explained.

Everyone watched on as the cop cars pulled away one after the other. The small gathering of people started to disperse and everyone returned to their homes as Alvin and Desi returned to their car and headed back to Martha's house.

"What happened?" Zoe asked anxiously when she opened the door to let Desi and Alvin in. It was apparent that she was still very shaken and now she was concerned with retribution. If the well intentioned visit from her friends further pissed Ramon off, what would he do to her now? How long would it be before he came after her and what wickedness would he inflict upon her?

"Don't worry, we didn't really get a chance to say anything to him," Desi began to explain. "By the time we arrived the cops had him cuffed and were escorting him out of the house, and that guy, Harvey, was in the back of an ambulance."

"Oh damn, what happened to Harvey? Is he going to be okay?" Zoe immediately knew that whatever fate Harvey had suffered was because he'd defended her.

"Apparently that thug you've been living with and his friend, Rich, beat the poor guy and tossed him into the street. Dude was pretty banged up, but because of him, Ramon is facing charges," Alvin explained.

"Zoe, the cops told me that if you go and file a report they can charge him for what he did to you," Desi spoke gently and encouragingly. "I can drive you down there right now. Additional charges will help keep Ramon's ass locked up a little longer."

"Do you know what he'll do to me if he finds out that I pressed charges against him? You have to understand, it's not just my safety I'm worried about. He's threatened to hurt Mama and Pam too," Zoe's voice trembled.

This is a situation that normally would have had Pam shaking in her boots, but she surprised everyone when she declared, "To hell with his threats, Zoe, you need to go press charges…now!"

Martha agreed whole-heartedly, but still Zoe opted to remain at her mother's, vowing to file charges first thing in the morning. Unfortunately, there was nothing that anyone could say to influence her to go to the police right then. Instead, she went and took a long hot shower, had a glass of wine, and went to bed. It had been one of the most horrific days of her life and she wasn't mentally prepared to divulge the gory details to some stranger. Besides, Ramon wouldn't be going anywhere before morning, that she was sure of.

CHAPTER TWENTY-EIGHT

Desi hadn't bothered to go home the night before. He slept on the couch so that when Zoe woke he could escort her to the police station. But it was now noon, Martha had made coffee and the two of them had been chatting at the kitchen table for a while. "She must really be wiped out, Ms. Martha, because it's not like Zoe to sleep this late," Desi remarked.

"I think it's more of a mental drain than anything. I know for a fact that Zoe never imagined she'd be in a situation like this. Once Otis was locked up, she vowed that no man would ever lay hands on her in a violent way. She thought that she could spot an abuser a mile away and knew what type of man she needed to avoid. All of this has shaken my baby to the core."

"I know, but I think that filing charges and taking an active role in Ramon's prosecution will be a great start to her reclaiming her power. He tried to beat her down, but it's time for her to take her life back."

"I'm going to check on her, see if she wants me to fix her something to eat." Martha pushed away from the table and padded down the hall to Zoe's bedroom. To her dismay, Zoe's bed was made and she was nowhere to be found. Martha hurried back to the front room and looked out the window. The parking space that housed Zoe's car last night was now occupied by someone else's truck. "Desi, she gone…" she announced when she rushed back to the kitchen.

Desi ran to the front window to see for himself as if Martha's words weren't believable. "Damn it, where could she be?" He asked out loud although there was no one there to provide an answer. "Ms. Martha, do you think she could be with Pam?"

"No, Pam tiptoed out this morning and went on to work."

Desi whipped out his cell phone and frantically dialed Zoe's number. When she didn't answer, his pressed end and then dialed April. She answered on the second ring and Desi wasted no time with pleasantries. "April, did Zoe show up at work today?"

"No, she called in early this morning, said she was sick and would be taking the rest of the week off. Is everything okay?"

"No, there was a situation with her and Ramon last night and now we don't know where she is."

"Shit! Have you tried to call Ramon?"

"He was actually locked up last night so there is no chance she's with him. But let me go and I promise that as soon as I find out where she is, I'll give you a call back." Desi disconnected the call, grabbed his keys and got ready to leave. "Ms. Martha, I'm going to ride by Ramon's and make sure that she didn't go by there for anything. As soon as I find her I'll give you a call."

Ramon's house was only a few blocks away and no more than a fifteen minute ride, but today the drive seemed to take an eternity. Desi played every possible scenario of what could've happened to Zoe over and over in his head. Had Ramon had someone else go after her, was she in an accident, did she try to run without telling anyone? Nothing he imagined was good and he was now terrified for his friend. He turned on Ramon's street and was torn between disappointment and relief when he saw that Zoe's car wasn't there. Still, he jumped out of his car and banged on the door to be absolutely sure that she wasn't inside. When there was no answer, he plopped down on the door step frustrated. Just as he dropped his head in his hands ready to give up, his cell phone rang. "Hello…"

"Hey Desi. Sorry I missed your call, but they took my phone," Zoe said all chipper as if she didn't have a care in the world.

"Who took your phone?"

"Security did, they don't allow cell phones in the police station," she explained.

"You've been to the police station? Why didn't you wake me so that I could go with you? Don't you know that I've been worried out of my mind?" The questions flew out of Desi's mouth so fast that Zoe could hardly keep up with all he'd asked.

"I'm sorry. I didn't mean to worry you; I just wanted to come down here on my own. I lay in bed all night thinking of how I'd released so much of my power to this idiot Ramon. Filing this report on my own was my way of taking some of that power back. You know, my way of standing up to him without fear of being smacked back down."

Desi breathed a sigh of relief, stood up, and walked to his car. "I understand and I'm proud of you for it. I just wished you would've let us know so we didn't go crazy worrying about you. Oh and you need to call your mama, she's worried out of her mind."

"Okay, but since you're there with her why can't you just tell her that I'm fine?" Zoe asked as she maneuvered her car out of the parking lot.

"Girl, I drove over here to Ramon's trying to see if maybe you'd come back for something."

"Oh, sorry about that, but since you're there can you hang out for a few minutes until I can get there? Ramon will be able to bond out soon and I want to grab as much of my stuff as I can before he does. I don't want to have to go back that way once he's out."

"No problem," Desi said as he turned off the ignition,

cracked a window, and relaxed into his leather seat. "Now call your mama."

Twenty minutes later, Zoe pulled in and parked in the driveway. When she knocked on Desi's window, he almost jumped out of his skin. "Girl, don't be sneaking up on people like that," he scolded as he stepped out of the car.

"Dude, you really shouldn't fall asleep in your car like that. I mean anyone could walk up on you, it's just not safe," she warned with a snicker. "Now come on, let's load up the cars and get the hell out of here."

Zoe slid the key in the lock and swung the door open. She immediately flashed back to the events of the previous night and it was enough to make her throw up. But she pulled herself together and escorted Desi to the master bedroom so that they could retrieve her clothes and other personal items. But to her dismay, the bulk of her things were nowhere to be found. Some of her jewelry was scattered on the floor, as were a few of her bras, panties, purses, and a couple of articles of clothing. Desi could see her body trembling and placed an arm around her waist in an effort to lend support. "Take a breath, honey, maybe he packed it all into garbage bags," he tried to reassure her.

"Maybe you're right. Let's check the rest of the house and see if we can find my stuff."

Zoe turned and walked to the kitchen, but there was no evidence of her belongings. She couldn't imagine what Ramon had done with her things. But then Desi opened the glass sliding door that led to the back yard and the mystery was solved. Almost everything Zoe owned was stuffed in metal trashcans and soaked in gasoline. She couldn't believe it, that son-of-a-bitch was going to burn everything she owned. His arrest must have been the reason he hadn't been able to actually send everything up in flames. But it didn't matter; the gas alone was enough to destroy the clothes. Desi looked at the trashcans in dismay, unable to understand how someone could be so low down. His eyes moved to Zoe and he waited for her to breakdown crying.

He was prepared to console her, but there would be no need for that. Her reaction was not the sadness he'd imagined it would be.

"If this is the cost of being rid of that jackass then it's a price I'm glad to pay. Hell, I needed a reason to go shopping anyway. Come on let's get the hell out of here." Zoe turned and headed back towards the kitchen. But before she could cross the threshold, someone else appeared in the yard. "Candy, what are you doing here?"

"Who the hell is she?" Desi asked bluntly.

"This is Rich's girlfriend and of course Rich is the asshole that got locked up with Ramon last night," Zoe answered. "So, Candy, what brings you out here?" She asked again.

Candy moved her right hand behind her back as if to hide something. "I just came by to see if you were here and to ask why you would press charges against Rich? Whatever happened between you and Ramon had nothing to do with my man."

"Are you serious?" For your information Candy, your man tried to ram his nasty ass penis down my throat last night. He is a freaking evil bastard and I don't understand why in the hell you have stayed with him all these years."

As Zoe and Candy went at each other, Desi moved around so that he could see what Candy was hiding behind her back and was shocked to see one of the long lighters used to ignite a fire in a grill. He stepped closer and yanked it out of her hand. "What were you going to do with this?" he asked rhetorically.

"Oh my gosh, you were coming over here to set my stuff on fire Candy?" Zoe asked in disbelief. "Are you ready to join them in jail? Because burning my property carries a destruction of personal property charge dumb ass."

"Okay, I know you're upset and I'm sorry for everything that happened to you last night, but there is no need for you to start calling me names. I didn't do anything to you and I won't stand here and be dogged by you," Candy's voice trembled as she spoke. It was almost as if she were this meek little girl on the verge of tears.

Zoe and Desi looked at each other in a semi state of confusion. It was clear that Candy wasn't capable of handling a serious confrontation. "Candy, I'm not trying to dog you," Zoe assured her. "But I do want to know why you would come over here to torch my stuff and how did you find out so quickly that I filed charges?"

"Rich called me from jail, said one of the jail employees told him you'd just left and had filed charges against him and Ramon. He was so pissed Zoe. He told me to come over here and light the stuff in the trashcans."

"You didn't question him, didn't tell him that you didn't want to trash my stuff?"

"Are you crazy! Haven't you learned that you don't question what Rich says, you just do what you're told. The quicker you learn that the better off you'll be," Candy advised.

"Why is that? Even Ramon does what Rich says. It's like he's got y'all trained or something." Zoe was trying to figure out why Rich had so much power over everybody.

"Of course Ramon is going to do what Rich says, Rich is his brother," Candy explained.

"No, Ramon told me that he had a brother, but after his adoptive family moved him down here he never saw his brother again."

"Rich found out where Ramon had moved and found a way to get down here too. He said that Ramon was the only family he had left and there was no way he'd allow anyone to separate them."

Zoe was feeling overwhelmed by everything. At this point all she wanted was to get the hell out of there and to the sanctity of her mother's home. "You know what Candy? You can burn the whole damn house down for all I care. I'm out of here and what I know for sure is that I'll never return. Lets' go Desi." She turned to walk away and Desi followed close behind.

"You'll be back," Candy mumbled. "You'll be back or you'll be dead."

Stunned, Zoe stood in place, took a deep breath and replied, "No I won't and if you had the sense God gave a gnat you'd take this opportunity to leave too. They're both locked up and I'm going to do everything in my power to keep it that way."

CHAPTER TWENTY-NINE

It would be less than a half hour before Pam arrived at Alvin's house. He was more nervous than he'd imagined he would be. Yes, he saw Pam all the time, she spent the night quite often and their love making was now a regular event that she had become totally comfortable with. Hell, she was even becoming more adventurous in the bedroom. But despite all of that, he had never asked her to marry him. As a matter of fact, he'd never asked anyone to marry him. In his mind and heart, no one had ever been worthy until now. In his eyes, Pam was an exceptional woman. She'd been through hell and back, worked through her issues, and become one of the strongest women he'd ever known. Her new found confidence was incredibly sexy. He found her to be very attractive, of course, but that's not what he loved most about her. Her heart, soul, honesty, vulnerability, strength and intelligence drew her closer to his heart with the passing of each day. So much so that he could no longer imagine his life without Pam Shaw.

Pam's session with Shellie was almost over. She'd shared with her therapist all that was going on with Zoe and how much she feared for her sister. But one thing Shellie took note of was that of all the things Pam had mentioned, Otis hadn't been one of them and Shellie viewed that as a victory. Pam had allowed her concern for others and her relationship with Alvin to take center stage in her life. She was no longer giving Otis power or top billing in her life. Otis had thankfully been moved to the back burner.

"I couldn't help but notice that of all the things and people we've discussed today, Otis wasn't a part of any of it," Shellie noted.

"You know Shellie; there are bigger issues right now. My greatest concern and biggest source of happiness have nothing to do with that drunken loser and everything to do with my sister, mother, and Alvin. Besides, I haven't seen him or the person that so strongly resembled him. I'm starting to think that it was all in my head. And quite honestly, even if it were Otis and if I saw him again today, I'd probably spit in his face instead of run and hide," Pam said boldly.

"I have never been more proud of anyone than I am of you right now Pam. You are truly an overcomer and an example to women everywhere. Do you realize how many abused women struggle for years and years before they're able to make as much progress as you have? You should be really proud of yourself," Shellie gushed like a proud mama bragging about her baby.

"I am proud," Pam smiled. "But I do have to admit that I am a little afraid about something else."

"And what would that be?"

"I think Alvin is going to ask me to move in with him and I'm not sure if I can do that."

"It is a big step Pam, but why the hesitation? I mean from what I understand you're already spending the night quite often."

"Yes I do, but I don't know if Mama is ready to live all alone. Her life is work, an occasional luncheon with Alvin's mom, and home. She won't consider dating and with me gone, I imagine she'd be mighty lonely."

Shellie tapped her pen on her notepad and glanced out the

window at the downtown skyline. "Pam, I never share my personal life with my patients, but I will share this with you. After my father and older sister died, my mom moved in with me. We stayed together for six years and I didn't allow myself to branch out too far away from her. I didn't think she'd be able to go on without me. But then I met my husband, we fell in love and I realized that I couldn't give up my life for my mother. That's a sacrifice no child should ever have to make. And once I married and moved out, my mom began to be more social with the folks in her community and even started doing volunteer work. She found herself and is happier than she's been in a very long time. Now you have to give your mom the chance to find herself. You have to live for yourself and give your mom the opportunity to do the same."

"I know that you're right, but part of me wonders if I'm the one who's not prepared to live separately from her," Pam confessed. She took a deep breath and exhaled slowly. "But you know if he asks and I say yes, I can always go running back to Mama if it doesn't work. I mean it's not like we're getting married," she chuckled.

Pam had been listening to her favorite Peace, Love, Music playlist as she drove to Alvin's. He'd asked her to come straight over after her session and she imagined that tonight would be the night he popped the big 'move in' question. But she was ready for it, she'd been thinking about everything Shellie had said and in her heart she knew that waking up with Alvin everyday would thrill her. She even went as far as practicing how she'd say yes as she drove to his neighborhood and the closer she got to his house, the more excited she became. In no time, Pam was whipping her car into Alvin's driveway and was all prepared to change her and her mother's life for the love of her man.

As she approached the door Alvin opened it just enough to allow her entry. The lights were dim, the music of Chris Botti filled the air, red roses were placed throughout, and she was greeted with a flute of champagne. Pam was very moved by all the trouble that Alvin had gone through to set the mood for the evening. As she looked around and then back at Alvin, her heart seemed to spill over with love. "To what do I owe this surprise?" she asked softly.

"You owe it to the fact that I love you," Alvin replied as he gently kissed her lips. He was a little surprised that Pam almost immediately began to kiss him more aggressively, more passionately. It was clear to see that she was ready to take things straight to the bedroom. It wasn't the way Alvin had planned, but only a fool would stop a woman as beautiful, and now, as sensual as Pam from getting the love she was craving.

The flutes were now empty and sitting on the coffee table and Pam was seductively undressing for her man. She slowly removed her blouse and skirt and stood proudly before Alvin in a lace bra, thong, and stilettos. Alvin was amazed by her incredible body and was unable to hide his excitement. The bulge in his pants was a dead giveaway of just how much he wanted her and how turned on he was by her boldness. Until now, Pam hadn't felt comfortable with Alvin seeing her so close to naked, but now she seemed to revel in it. She stepped to Alvin confidently and gently nibbled at his lips as she undressed him. When his pants dropped to the floor, Pam dropped to her knees. She was a little nervous because she'd never done this before, but Alvin was excited beyond belief. She first licked his manhood gently, circling the tip with her tongue before taking him into her mouth. With each motion of her head she took in more and more of him and his moans were confirmation that she was doing something right. When she felt his leg begin to tremble, she slowly stood to her feet and kissed him passionately. He returned her kisses as he removed her bra and set her beautiful breasts free. Just the sight of her erect nipples made his heart race a little faster. He moved his kisses to her breasts, sucking and licking on one, then the other. Her heavy breathing was like her signature on the permission slip that allowed him to go further. Alvin laid her down on the sofa, spread her legs, and began to feast on her love. The more he licked and sucked the more her juices flowed. Pam had never felt anything as good as what she was feeling now. Her body shivered and pelvic muscles contracted until she'd experienced the orgasm of a lifetime. But yet she still wanted more, she wanted to feel Alvin inside of her and he was more than happy to oblige. He entered her ever so gently, but quickly began to increase the force and speed of his motion and in her excitement, she matched his every movement. The explosion of their climax was epic.

After catching their breath, the couple made their way to the bedroom where they relaxed into each other's arms. Alvin kissed Pam on the forehead and spoke softly, "Baby, I want to ask you something." A smile spread across her face because in her mind she knew exactly what he was about to ask. "You know I love you baby and every day I'm grateful that you came into my life. We've grown so close, so much so that I can't imagine my life without you." He maneuvered his body so that he was looking down into her eyes. "Pam, what I'm trying to ask is…will you marry me?"

Pam was stunned and trying to figure out if she heard him correctly. The words 'Did he just say marry?' echoed in her head. This was not what she had planned for and honestly, not at all what she wanted. Pam's desire was for a committed relationship and she felt that they already had that and didn't need a stupid piece of paper confirm it. Her mind was flying as she tried to figure out the best way to respond.

"Baby, what do you say? Will you marry me?" Alvin asked again as he tried to figure out what her hesitation was all about.

Pam reached her hand up and gently caressed his face. Her eyes filled with tears and she smiled at him so sweetly. "I love you so much Alvin and my life has improved tenfold since you walked into it. You are without a doubt the best thing that's ever happened to me, but marriage is huge, it's a bigger move than I ever imagined I'd make."

Alvin looked as if he'd been punched in the gut. He sat up in bed and Pam did the same. With his voice cracking from disappointment, he asked, "So are you saying you don't want to be with me long term? Is this just a temporary fling to you?"

"No! That is absolutely not what I'm saying. You are my heart and I want to spend the rest of my life with you, just not as your wife. I fully expected for you to ask me to move in with you and I was totally prepared to say yes. I'd love to live here with you so that we can build a life together, but we don't need a marriage certificate to do that."

"Pam, I want a wife not a roommate." Alvin reached back and grabbed a jewelry box from the nightstand drawer. He opened the top to reveal a magnificent emerald cut diamond ring. Pam was in awe of how lovely it was and when he slid it on her finger she couldn't help but look at her hand with new found admiration. "Tell me that you want more Pam; tell me that you'll be my wife."

"Alvin, tell me that we can live happily ever after without the marriage vows," she pleaded.

"I can't do that. Shacking up is not enough for me."

"And marriage is too much for me."

CHAPTER THIRTY

Zoe was feeling confident and free knowing that Ramon was no longer a part of her life. The charges that had been filed against him in conjunction with her past complaints were surely enough to keep him locked up until his trial date, or so she thought. But a visit with Harvey would completely change all of that. She'd gone by the hospital to thank him for coming to her defense and apologize for the beating he'd suffered because of her. She quietly entered his room carrying a beautiful bouquet of flowers. She thought he was asleep, but slowly he turned his head in her direction and smiled when he realized who had come to see him.

"Hey there Zoe. What are you doing here?"

"I came to pay my knight in shining armor a visit. How are you?" she asked as she took notice of his swollen and bruised left eye, arm cast, and tube that appeared to be attached to his chest.

"I'll live I suppose, but I have to admit, they got me good."

"Was any permanent damage done?" Zoe asked hesitantly.

"Nah, the worst injury is the punctured lung. Apparently they broke a couple of ribs and that caused the puncture. But the doctors put in a chest tube for drainage and it should heal just fine. How are you?"

"I'm fine…" her voice trailed off as she tried to hold back

her tears. "Harvey, saying thank you seems so inadequate for what you did for me. I truly believe that you saved my life and I am more appreciative than you'll ever know," Zoe said as she wiped the tears she was no longer able to hold back. "If there is anything that I can do to help you just say the word. I'm glad to reimburse as much as I can of the salary you'll miss during your recuperation."

"Zoe, that's not necessary and you don't owe me a thing. If anyone is owed something it's you. I'm sorry that I let it go on as long as I did. Rich and Ramon are a couple of heathens, they're sick," Harvey spat in disgust. "Please, whatever you do, stay the hell away from Ramon once he's released. If I were you, I'd seriously consider moving so that he won't know where to find you or your family."

"Is that really necessary? I mean they won't be getting out of jail anytime soon. The assault charges are not exactly misdemeanors."

"No they're not, but those two have a stash of cash and unless they're given a million dollar cash bond, they'll be able to get out," Harvey informed her as he watched the color drain from her face.

"Where did they get that kind of money and is it true that they are brothers?"

"How did you find out they're brothers? I mean there are only a couple of people that know and even fewer know that before Rich moved here to find his brother, he was a drug dealer. He made a ton of money and when the cops got on his tail, he packed his bags and his money and headed south."

Zoe shook her head in disgust. Of all the men in Atlanta, how had she allowed herself to get involved with the likes of Ramon? She thought she knew how to read all the signs, how to differentiate between an abusive man and a good one. But her instincts had failed her or maybe she'd just failed to follow her instincts. Either way, it was time for her to make some serious changes and as much as she hated to put her family through it, they would have to suffer through the changes as well. The thought of it all weighed heavily on her and she no longer tried to wipe away the tears or hide her emotion. "Harvey, I don't know how I could've been so stupid. I'm supposed to be a better judge of character," she sobbed.

"There was no way for you to know Zoe. Trust me, they have perfected their game. Rich learned from his father and he passed all the sadistic lessons on to Ramon. They treat their women like queens at first and once they're sure the women love them, they flip on them. It's like they'll beat these girls into submission, threaten them until they're too scared to take a shit without permission."

"Is that what happened to Candy?"

"Yep, Rich has beaten the poor girl into complete submission. I swear she'll do anything for him, she'd kill herself if he told her to."

"Yeah, she actually came by Ramon's house to set all my stuff on fire because those clowns called her from jail and told her to. She told me either I'd go back to Ramon or I'd be dead."

"No Zoe, you won't die at his hands, but if you go back I swear I'll kill you my damn self. Now before they get released go find yourself somewhere else to live. He won't bother you at work, he's too smart to make a public scene, but if he knows where you live, he'll show up and try to torture you for the fun of it. Now I'll be out of here in a couple of days, so jot down my number and if you need me just call me. I'll always do anything I can to protect you from that damn Ramon."

Zoe gave him a sweet, appreciative smile and kiss on the cheek. "Thank you for everything Harvey and I'll check on you soon."

* * *

Martha hadn't blinked twice when Zoe relayed all that Harvey had shared with her, including his advice that they move. All she'd said was "Let's go to U-Haul and get some boxes and tape." Zoe was so sorry that her mom had to be uprooted again, but was thankful that Martha was so understanding and supportive. Martha had even remarked that she wished she had been as strong as her girls when she was younger. If she'd had the strength and courage to leave Otis, their lives would've been so different. But there was no way for her to change any of that now and to dwell on it was pointless. Now was the time to do all that she could to help keep her daughters safe. Martha had taken it upon herself to go out and purchase a 9mm gun for protection. She'd even gone so far as to take her new weapon to the shooting range for lessons. Her thought process now was that if someone was big and bad enough to burst in her home, then they were big and bad enough to take a bullet.

Now the only thing left to do was to tell Pam that they had to move. Martha decided to deliver the news herself. She didn't know how Pam would react, but thought she could better handle her hysterics than Zoe could. Zoe had always had a way with Pam, but now she was so shaken that handling her older sister just wasn't an option. Martha patiently sat at the kitchen table, sipped on coffee, and waited for Pam to get home. She'd spent the night with Alvin so Martha had expectations of Pam being in a great mood, but she was dead wrong. When Pam finally made it home, she walked in the kitchen, dropped her hand bag, and plopped down. She looked as if she'd been crying.

What now? "What's wrong, baby?" Martha asked hesitantly.

"Alvin asked me to marry him last night," Pam said flatly.

"Pam that is wonderful," Martha clapped her hands as if she were staring in a Clump's movie. Then she realized she was the only one that was excited. "What's wrong? I would think that you'd be jumping up and down with excitement. Why are we not celebrating?"

"Mama, I don't want to get married. I told you that a long time ago, remember? I've been clear that marriage is not something I've ever wanted for myself. I do want a committed relationship, but I don't think a piece of paper is necessary in order to have that. I told him that I'd love to move in and share his life and space, but he said that's not enough."

"Sweetheart, do you know how many women would kill to be in your position? You have a wonderful man that loves you and wants to build a life with you. Please help me to understand why you don't want that?"

"I do want that Mama, but you don't have to be married to build a life with someone. Everyone I've ever known that's had a good relationship lost it after they got married. Marriage changes things Spouses take each other for granted, fight about every little thing, and sadly, they stop trying to please each other. Married people tend to think about themselves first, their spouse last, and complain about everything. That's not the kind of relationship I want."

"It doesn't have to be that way for you and Alvin. Yes, I'm the first to admit that marriage is hard, but contrary to popular belief there are some beautiful marriages out there. There are still men that respect their wives, are faithful, loving, and dedicated to being good family men."

"And he can be all that without being married! Hell, look at Oprah and Stedman, they've been together for years and have never needed a marriage license to prove that they are dedicated to one another," Pam's voice spiked with frustration.

"What's going on?" Zoe asked as she entered the room. She assumed that the tension she felt was because Pam had been advised of their pending move.

"Alvin asked your sister to marry him last night and she said no," Martha said with a bit of an attitude.

"Humph… Well congratulations on the proposal and the courage it took to say no." Zoe grabbed a soda out of the fridge and joined them at the table.

"How can you two be so cavalier about being single for the rest of your lives?" Martha clearly didn't understand that every woman didn't have grand dreams of marriage and kids floating in their heads.

"Mama, I've seen enough horrible marriages to know that it's something I'd have to think long and hard about before agreeing to be any man's wife. Hell, I don't even think I'd agree to even living with anyone else at this point," Zoe confessed.

"Zoe, you're upset about everything that's happened to you and just speaking out of anger. But Pam, Alvin is a wonderful man and I'd hate to see you lose him and the wonderful life y'all could have together."

"I hear you Mama," Pam quipped. "So enough about me, what else is going on?"

Martha and Zoe exchanged glances and Pam knew that whatever would follow wouldn't be good. "Are y'all going to keep cutting your eyes at each other or is somebody going to open their mouth and tell me something?"

"I'm sorry Pam, but we've got to move," Zoe said bluntly and she could see shock and anger creep across Martha's face.

They'd agreed that the news would be better delivered by Martha, but Zoe had dropped it like it was nothing. And to their great surprise, Pam didn't flip out, didn't cry, didn't start shaking, or checking the locks. She simply said "Yeah, I figured we would."

CHAPTER THIRTY-ONE

April had been blowing Zoe's phone up. She was worried about her friend and knew that something bad had happened, but Desi never called her back. Zoe had been so caught up in the mess that was her life that she hadn't returned any of Aprils calls. Finally they'd gotten a chance to talk in depth over lunch and April was shocked, but more than anything she was mad as hell. She'd never understood how a man could be so weak as to put his hands on a woman, let alone do the evil that Ramon had done to Zoe. When Zoe told her that she had to quickly find a place to move to, April placed a call, wrote down an address, and told Zoe to bring her sister and mom there after work.

Seven o'clock rolled around and the Shaw women were pulling into the driveway of a nice split level house just east of downtown Atlanta. The neighborhood was well kept and all the lawns were perfectly manicured. "Whose house is this?" Pam asked.

"I'm not sure. This is where April said for us to meet her. Let me call her and see where she is." Zoe reached for her cell phone, but as she got ready to dial the number a car pulled up behind her. Zoe glanced in the rearview mirror and saw a gorgeous specimen of a man step out of the driver's seat. The tall, mocha colored man walked around, opened April's door and extended his hand for her to grab onto. Zoe jumped out of the car anxious to see who April was with and why she had them meet her there.

"Hi ladies," April chirped cheerfully. "This is my brother, Eugene. Eugene, this is my friend, Zoe, her mother, Martha, and sister, Pam.

"Wow, a family of beautiful women," Eugene remarked as he shook each of their hands. "It's a real pleasure to meet you all."

"It's nice to meet you as well," Zoe said with a smile on her face. She then turned her attention to April. "So April, what are we doing here girl? Whose house is this?"

"It's yours if you want it," April replied matter-of-factly. "Eugene here owns several residential properties in and around the city. I told him a little about your situation and he has offered to let you guys rent this house for as long as you want to."

"Are you serious?" Zoe's smile grew wider and when she looked at Martha and Pam, they too were grinning like little kids. "Do you mind if we look around inside?"

"Yes we're serious and feel free to look around as much as you like," Eugene confirmed as he held out a set of keys to Zoe.

The house was beautiful. There was a large eat-in kitchen, living room, formal dining room, family room, and three spacious bedrooms. But the best part for Zoe was that there was a finished basement. For her that meant creating her own living space and regaining the privacy that she hadn't had since leaving Virginia. She mentally mapped out how she would decorate it, what would go where, and how peaceful it would be.

"Eugene, how much are you asking for rent?" Martha asked.

"Is $1000 per month plus utilities reasonable for you guys?"

"Are you kidding? That's less than what we're paying now for that cramped apartment we're in!" Pam couldn't hide her excitement.

"Wait Eugene, we appreciate this so much, but we're not

trying to take advantage. You could easily get much more than that for this house."

"You're not taking advantage," he reassured her. "You'll actually be doing me a favor, this house has been sitting for a while and I don't like for my properties to be empty for too long."

"Are you sure?" Zoe asked with concern written on her face.

"He's positive Zoe, now stop looking a gift horse in the mouth," April interjected. "Now when do y'all want to move in?"

"Is tomorrow too soon?" Martha asked. She had been packing like a mad woman and was anxious to move. The last thing she wanted was for Ramon to get out before they could relocate.

"I'll have a moving truck at your apartment in the morning," Eugene replied with a smile, displaying his gorgeous pearly whites again.

"Eugene you don't have to do that, we can"

Agitated, April interrupted, "Damn Zoe. Let the man do this for y'all if he wants. You need to learn to let people help you and just say thank you."

Everyone had taken off work and helped in the move. After everything was situated, Zoe ran out and grabbed food and wine so that they could celebrate their new place. April, Desi, Kirk, and Alvin had all pitched in. Despite being upset over Pam's rejection of his proposal, when he found out about the move, Alvin was the first one in line to help. They stayed up all night to finish the packing and waited at the house for the boxes and furniture to be delivered. Zoe shed tears as she watched everyone lift a celebratory toast. Despite everything she'd been through, she was grateful for her friends and family and didn't know how she'd make it without them. She was also grateful that her supervisor had approved her request for family leave. Now she would have time to get her house and life in order as well as protect the job she'd come to love. At that moment, Zoe knew that God was changing things in her life and bringing her out of the darkness.

CHAPTER THRIRTY-TWO

Less than two weeks after their initial arrest, Ramon and Rich walked out of jail like they didn't have a care in the world. Candy was sitting outside of the Fulton County Police Department waiting to pick them up. "Hey guys, do you all want to go grab something to eat?" she asked in hopes that she could distract Ramon from the revenge that she knew must've been on his mind.

"Hey Candy. I'll leave y'all to the feasting. Would you please just drop me off at my house?"

"Sure," she replied very unenthusiastically.

"Why you sound so disappointed, my company ain't good enough for you?" Rich asked as he grabbed her thigh and squeezed tightly.

Candy winced in pain. "Of course you are baby. I didn't mean to sound like that. I'm always happy to be alone with you," she lied.

"That's my girl," Rich leaned in with a kiss and released the vice grip he had on her leg. "Now what are you going to fix to eat when we get home?"

"I thought we'd go out and get something really good. Maybe eat at Rosebuds since we both love the food there."

"I want you in some heels, one of those short nighty things, and in the kitchen cooking me some pork chops," Rich spoke in a harsh tone letting her know that that was his final decision.

Candy remained silent for the rest of the ride to Ramon's house. But she listened intently as he spoke of how he was going to immediately jump in his truck, go to Martha's, and yank Zoe's ass out of there. The more he talked the angrier he became. Ramon was pissed not only at the fact that Zoe left, but also that she had the nerve to press charges against him. For him, that was the ultimate betrayal and he had big plans to make her regret ever having done it. Candy's heart began to ache for Zoe. She knew that Rich had probably concocted some wicked, painful punishment and Ramon was more than ready to inflict it upon her. Candy pulled in the driveway and before she could come to a complete stop, Ramon had opened the door, ready to jump out.

"Alright man, go get that bitch and make her pay for this shit," Rich encouraged him.

"I'll call you later and see if you want to come over and join in the fun," Ramon grinned sadistically as he closed the car door and went to get in his truck.

Ramon peeled out of the driveway and hurried over to Martha's apartment. He didn't see Zoe's car there, but that didn't mean anything. With Pam and Martha sharing a car now, one of them could have borrowed Zoe's. He rushed past a couple of older men and jumped up the stairs two at a time. Ramon banged on the door as if he were trying to knock it down. His frustration began to grow when no one bothered to answer.

"Zoe, Martha, Pam, one of y'all need to open the door now!" he demanded, but still his knocks went unanswered. "Look, I just want to talk Zoe, I promise," he continued. He spun around to scan the parking lot once more, hoping that he'd just missed her car and she really was inside cowering in a corner. But there was no car, just one of the old men starring up at him as if he wanted to kill him. "What the hell are you looking at?" he barked at the man.

"A dumb ass fool," the man responded bluntly. "And they moved."

"When? Do you know where they moved to?" Ramon shouted as he ran back down the stairs.

"I'm sure if the ladies wanted you to know that they would have told you," the old man responded.

"Look old man, I got $50 for you if you can tell me when and where they moved," Ramon bribed.

"Boy, you don't have enough money to make me tell you nothing," he grumbled as he turned his back to walk away. Ramon reached out and grabbed the man by the shoulder. "Boy, get your hands off of me. I'm not one of these women that you can smack around. I'm a grown man and I won't hesitate to put a bullet in your ass." The man snatched his shoulder from Ramon's grip and walked away.

Ramon was dumbfounded by the old man and his unwillingness to give up any information. He sprinted back to his truck and took off. If they had moved, he knew that Desi would know exactly where to find them. As he pulled up to Desi's place he spotted Kirk and Desi getting into a car and pulled in behind them blocking their exit. He threw the truck into park and jumped out in a huff. "Desi, where can I find Zoe?"

"Man, get the hell out of the way so that we can leave," Desi demanded.

"Look, I didn't come here to make trouble," Ramon said as he humbled himself. "I just want to find Zoe and apologize. I love her and I don't know what the hell I was thinking when I hurt her. All I want is to make it right." The lies tumbled from his mouth like mud in a landslide.

"You should have thought about all of that beforehand. She wants nothing to do with you and if you go near her again your ass will be back in jail in the blink of an eye. Now move that raggedy ass truck out the way." Desi turned to get in the car when he saw Kirk jump out with a bat in hand.

"Touch him and I'll beat the living hell out of you!" Kirk warned when he saw Ramon move aggressively towards Desi.

"You punk! You were going to jump me from behind? Damn, you can't even come at another dude face to face. Sneak attacks on men and beating women, damn you're a bigger coward than I thought you were. Ain't no way in hell I'll ever let you near Zoe again. Now get the hell out of here before I call the cops." Desi stood and watched as Ramon got back in his truck and pulled away.

Turning the corner, Ramon cursed as he hit his steering wheel. He knew that he needed to play it cool with Desi, but his hatred for the man and desperation to find Zoe got the better of him. But he wasn't ready to give up, he pulled just outside the gate and waited for Kirk and Desi to pull off and he'd follow them for a bit to see if they'd lead him to Zoe. Twenty minutes later and Ramon was more disgusted than ever to see that he'd been led to Bulldogs, the hottest gay club in Atlanta. Ramon couldn't see how Desi and Kirk laughed at him as he hurried off down the street.

Back at the house, Ramon looked around to see if there was any remnants of Zoe, but as he expected, everything had pretty much been destroyed. He sat alone thinking of the good times he'd shared with Zoe, how he loved seeing her prance around the house in his tee shirts. He remembered how she'd crawl into bed and lay on his chest. And the more Ramon traveled down memory lane, the angrier he became. How could she so easily have walked out on him? Sure they fought, but every couple fought. And the whole thing with Rich, it was just his way of teaching her a lesson. If she had just understood that it was her job to do what he wanted and not make a big deal out of every little situation, they could still be together, sharing a happy life. But no, her strong will and refusal to be the woman he wanted her to be had torn them apart. Her high and mighty ass had even been keeping a file of shit she thought he'd done wrong and was trying to use it to keep him locked away. "That bitch!" he screamed as he flipped over the coffee table and punched a hole in the wall with his fist. Pacing the floor in anger, he realized that by now she'd left work more than an hour ago. But that was okay, he was concocting a plan to get his hands on her before the weekend was over.

CHAPTER THIRTY-TWO

Martha was smiling ear to ear as she prepared Saturday morning breakfast for she and her girls. She'd made them help her unpack the kitchen before sorting things out in any other room. She loved the abundance of cabinets and all of the counter space. When she first stepped into the walk in pantry, she thought she'd died and gone to kitchen heaven. All of the appliances were new and state of the art, Eugene had even had a new side-by-side refrigerator delivered.

"It smells good in there Mama. How much longer before it's ready?" Zoe yelled from the family room.

"Another five or ten minutes and we'll be eating."

Zoe turned her attention back to unpacking and the conversation she was having with Pam. "Are you starting to regret turning down Alvin's proposal? I mean he is the best thing that's ever happened to you. He loves you unconditionally, is always there for you, and understands your past. Any girl would regret denying a man like that and of course, it's not too late to change your mind."

"Look, I respect and understand your views and opinions about Alvin and about our relationship. He is a wonderful man, no one can deny that, but I just don't want to get married. I don't understand why he is so against us living together in a committed relationship without that stupid piece of paper. I mean if it's good enough for Oprah then it should be good enough for us," Pam surmised.

"Oh my sweet sister, you are not Oprah. You are a woman scared to trust a man enough to fully commit to him, despite how he has proved himself worthy time and time again."

Pam stopped un wrapping the framed pictures and looked Zoe dead in the eyes. "So you can honestly stand there and tell me that with all you've been through, you'd still trust a man enough to marry him?"

"Yes, despite everything I still have high hopes for finding someone decent who will love, respect, and support me. It was hard to open up to Ramon and I regret that I did, but Alvin has inspired me. By loving you the way he has, he's shown me that there are some truly good men still left in the world and I hope that one day one of them will find me."

* * *

Rich burst into laughter as Ramon told him of his plan to find out where Zoe was now living. He told Rich how Zoe was always so worried for Candy because of the so called abuse she suffered at Rich's hand. It was Ramon's thinking that Zoe would be more than willing to help Candy escape the abuse that she was so sure she'd escaped.

"Man, if she moved it only makes sense that she changed her phone number too. So how will Candy call her?" Rich asked.

"That shows how stupid her ass is. She kept her number, but won't answer my calls. She sends my ass straight to voice mail."

"Okay, so this just might work," Rich stroked his chin as if he were some deep thinker. Then he shouted, "Candy, come here and hurry up."

Candy strolled into the room looking as if she didn't know whether to be scared or annoyed. "What is it?"

"Did Zoe ever give you her number?" Ramon quizzed.

"Yeah, she gave it to me a while back."

"What difference does that make? Even if she didn't have the number you've got it, boy genius," Rich remarked.

"If she never gave her number to Candy and Candy calls her out the blue, she'd know I was behind it, dumb ass," Ramon snapped.

"Forget you man, just tell this bitch what you want her to do."

"Look Candy, Zoe won't answer my calls and I don't know where she's living now. I need you to call her and act like you need her help. Tell her that Rich has hurt you and you want to get away from him. I know she'll want to help you, but you've got to sound convincing," Ramon emphasized.

Candy started to tear up and her bottom lip began to tremble. "Ramon, maybe you should just walk away. I…I…mean if she wants to be gone that bad, do you really even wa…want her back?" She stuttered, obviously scared of their reaction, but still wanting to protect Zoe.

"Yes I'm sure. Now make the call," Ramon tried to speak calmly.

"I just know that if someone wanted to be away from me that bad, I wouldn't even want them anymore. She's just not good enough for you anyway Ramon," Candy said as she made one last attempt to save Zoe from his wrath. But now it was Rich who had grown angry and impatient with her song and dance. He jumped up out of his chair and Candy knew that she was in trouble.

"Why the hell are you trying to save her ass?" Rich shouted as he struck Candy across the face with a backhand. The blood from her lip tasted a little salty. She'd hoped that would be the only strike, but deep down she knew better. "If you would just do as you're told, you'd save yourself a lot of pain." He landed another smack across the face, this time with his closed fist. And then another right to her left eye and she instantly felt it begin to swell. Grabbing her around her neck and squeezing tightly, Rich barked, "Now get your damn phone and call her now!" When he released his grip, Candy gasped for air and fumbled to pull her phone out of her pocket.

Sobbing, Candy dialed Zoe's number. To her surprise and disappointment, Zoe answered on the second ring. "Zoe, this is Candy. I need help."

"What's wrong, why are you crying? Did Rich hurt you?" The concern in her voice was unmistakable.

"Yes, Rich attacked me and I ran out when he fell asleep, but I don't have anywhere to go," Candy lied and sobbed.

Zoe hesitated for a moment, but her conscience wouldn't let her turn her back to Candy. If the woman ended up dead or something, Zoe would never be able to forgive herself. "Okay, can you get to the Starbucks around the corner from your house?"

"Yes, I'll be there waiting for you in a few minutes," Candy cried.

CHAPTER THIRTY-THREE

"Damn it, Zoe, I don't think you should go. She may be crying now but she's the same one that told you to go back to Ramon or die all while she was trying to set your shit on fire," Pam yelled. "Now I'm sorry that she's an abused woman, but you need to stay away from her. I mean what if Ramon is hiding in the background just waiting to pounce?"

"Pam, I know what that damn Rich is capable of and I can't in good conscience leave her there if she's crying for help. I won't be long, I promise I'll be okay and when I get back the three of us will head on out to dinner. Love y'all and I'll be back shortly," Zoe assured them as she headed out the door.

"Mama, why didn't you try to help me talk her out of going?" Pam asked as she plopped down on the couch.

"She is right, if something happened to that girl and she could've prevented it, she'd never live in peace again. The best thing we can do is pray for her safety and quick return," Martha advised. But deep in her heart she was scared to death for Zoe. It was all she could do to keep tears from rolling down her face. She loved her children and continued to blame herself for exposing them to a violent environment. Had she not, they would've lived totally different lives.

Zoe headed across town to the Starbucks and she prayed all the way. She asked God for guidance and most of all for protection. Within thirty minutes she was pulling into the parking lot where she saw a young woman sitting alone at one of the outdoor tables. Zoe parked the car and made her way over to the table. "Candy, is that you?" When the woman looked up and she saw how badly she'd been beaten, her heart sank. "Oh Candy, I'm so sorry he did this to you." Zoe sat down and wrapped an injured and weeping Candy in her arms. "Okay, he'll be up looking for you soon so let's get out of here. You can come home with me."

"No, I need you to listen to me," Candy sobbed. "This is a setup, Ramon and Rich are parked around the corner watching us. It's my job to get you to take me home with you so that they can follow and find out where you live. Ramon is determined to get you back and he's using me to do it."

"Damn it, is Ramon the one that beat you like this?"

"No, this was courtesy of Rich. He got pissed cause I was trying to talk Ramon out of trying to find you. Plus he thought that the bruises would convince you that I needed your help. He's such a bastard," Candy spat.

"Well I can't leave you here or Rich will kill you, but I can't let them know where I live either." Zoe's mind was flying as she tried to figure out her next move.

"Zoe, you're going to put your arm around me, walk me to your car and help me in. I need them to think that I'm really playing my role well. But instead of taking me to your home, you're going to drive me to the women's shelter over in midtown. When I get out of the car, you peel out of there. They are going to stop long enough for Rich to get me back in the truck. You'll have a little bit of a head start, but just in case it's not enough, go to one of your friend's houses and hang out for a while. They are not patient and if you stay for longer than thirty minutes or so, they're going to leave and then you can go home. You got all that?" Candy asked.

"This is un-freaking believable. How did I allow this to become my life," Zoe shook her head in disgust.

"Look, you can have your pity party later, but right now we need to go. Get up and act like you're helping me up and to the car."

Zoe did as she was told; she held Candy around the shoulders and escorted her to the car. As she walked to the driver's side of her car, she instinctively looked around to see if she saw Ramon and Rich lurking in the background. She didn't see them anywhere but didn't doubt for a second that they were watching her every move. Candy gave her the location of the shelter and she headed that way. "Candy, I can't thank you enough for this. It would've been so easy for you to mislead me. But I'm concerned for your wellbeing and how bad it will be for you later."

"I don't even care, Zoe. I figure the worst he can do is beat me again and the most merciful thing he could do is kill me. At least that way I wouldn't be tortured anymore."

Zoe didn't know what to say. How do you comfort someone who views a violent death as a viable escape plan? Instead of speaking, she reached over with her free hand and laid it on top of Candy's, but Candy moved her hand away. Human touch was not something she longed for anymore.

"You see that tan house right up there? That's the shelter. Remember what I said, take off as fast as you can and go hang out with a friend for a while," Candy instructed.

"Are you sure Candy? I don't want you hurt any more than you already are."

As the car came to a stop, Candy took a deep breath and replied, "I'm sure." She jumped out of the car and made a run for the front door of the shelter. Zoe had no idea if she made it or not because she hit the gas just like Candy had instructed. As Zoe flew through the city, she called Desi to let him know that she had an emergency and was on her way over. She kept looking in her rearview mirror and felt confident that Ramon had not been able to follow her. What she didn't realize was that Rich had jumped out of the truck, ran and yanked Candy back by the hair just before she skipped through the door. And to make matters worse, Ramon didn't wait on Rich and Candy, but instead he sped off to catch Zoe. Once he had her in sight, he stayed a couple of car lengths back to ensure that she didn't see him. He became incredibly irritated when he realized they'd driven to Desi's place, but he was determined to wait it out. Ramon stayed there for three hours watching people come and go. He saw the old man from Zoe's old apartment complex, the one that wouldn't tell him where or when Zoe had moved. He wondered to himself how many complexes could one man work for. He watched the women passing by and thought of the things he'd like to do to them. And finally, Zoe emerged from Desi's apartment. She trotted across the parking lot and unknowingly took off with Ramon hot on her tail.

After pulling into her driveway, Zoe sprinted to the door with keys in hand. She managed to get in and lock the door before Ramon could park and jump out of his truck. But in a matter of seconds he was banging on the front door demanding entry. Zoe stood in the living room shocked that he'd found her. She stood there shaking in her proverbial boots as Martha and Pam ran to the front room to see what the commotion was all about.

Bang, bang, bang... The door shook from the pounding. "Open the door, Zoe. I'm not leaving until you let me in. I just want five minutes to talk, that's all. Now open the door!" Bang, bang, bang, bang... The violent knocking was relentless. "Open the damn door, Zoe! I know you're in there. I saw you run in and your damn cars in the driveway."

"Ramon, get the hell out of here before I call the cops," Martha threatened.

"Ms. Martha, all I want to do is talk to Zoe for a minute, that's all. I'm not here to cause any trouble, but she owes me a conversation. The least she can do is give me five minutes."

"She doesn't owe you a damn thing," Pam shouted as she tightly held a butcher knife she'd grabbed from the kitchen before running to the front room.

Seeing Pam standing with a knife and speaking up so strongly in her defense snapped Zoe out of her trance. She knew she had to handle this situation so that it didn't escalate and become a greater threat to all of the Shaw women. "Ramon, I'm here but you need to know that I'm not going to open the door. Anything you want to say you can go head and say. I promise that I can hear you just fine," she assured him.

"Zoe, I'm not going to scream through this damn door, now I'm going to ask again as nicely as possible. Open the fucking door!"

His screeching demand sent chills down their backs and prompted Martha to make a run for the phone. But before she could reach the kitchen, Ramon kicked the door in and grabbed Zoe by the neck. "I told you to open the damn door."

"Let her go!" Pam demanded as she held the knife up, ready to plunge it into Ramon's back. "I said let her go!"

Ramon did as he was told and loosened his grip on Zoe's neck. But quicker than she expected, he turned his attention to Pam and attempted to grab the knife. She managed to slice through his hand before he knocked her out cold with the other. "Where is Martha?" Ramon asked as he watched Zoe rush to Pam's aid. "I said where is Martha?" He asked again as he kicked Zoe in her side.

"She ran out the back to our neighbor's house for help. You'd better leave before the cops get here," Zoe warned through hysterical tears.

"Your big ass mama ain't never ran nowhere," he grumbled as he grabbed Zoe by the arm and drug her through the house in search of Martha. He heard Martha in the kitchen reciting the address. He turned the corner and snatched the phone out of the wall. Zoe screamed as she watched Ramon bang her mother's head into the wall and Martha slid to the ground. "Come on, we're leaving," he announced as he tried to snatch Zoe up from the floor.

"Go to hell you son-of-a-bitch, I'm not going anywhere with you." Zoe scrambled to her feet and grabbed a glass that she threw at Ramon as she tried to run away. The glass barely missed his head and shattered against the wall. He wasted no time catching her and yanking her back by her hair. "Don't be stupid, Ramon, you know the cops are on their way," she tried to reason, but it was to no avail. He held her tightly by the back of the head and ushered her towards the front door. Pam was coming around and tried to get up to help her baby sister, but dizziness knocked her back down. Then Zoe remembered hearing that the biggest mistake one could make was to allow themselves to be taken to another location by their captor. Not knowing what else to do, she let her body go limp and fall to the floor. Ramon almost fell trying to hold her dead body weight up.

"What the hell are you doing? Get up, Zoe, get the hell up now!" he shouted as he tried to pull her to her feet. But when she refused to cooperate, he became enraged and pounded her in the face with his closed fist and she screamed out like a wounded animal. But before he could continue his attack on her, out of nowhere a metal pipe came down across his back and this time it was Ramon who squealed in pain. He stumbled back and when he looked up to see who his attacker was, he looked right into the eyes of the old man from the apartment complex. Ramon tried to charge the man, but when the man cracked him in the knee with the pipe, Ramon went down like a sack of potatoes.

"Oh my God, Otis?" Zoe couldn't believe her eyes. It was her father, Otis that had swung the pipe and stopped Ramon's attack on her. When Pam heard Zoe call his name, she looked up and almost lost all the courage and strength she'd gained. One look into Otis' face and Pam started crying silent tears but refused to scurry across the floor and ball herself up in a corner. Martha emerged from the kitchen and couldn't believe her eyes.

How the hell had Otis found them? As the Shaw women looked on in shock, Otis stood over Ramon daring him to move. Within seconds, the police sirens could be heard blaring down the street headed in their direction. Not only had Martha managed to call them, but the shouting and crying prompted the neighbors to call for help as well.

The cops rushed to the door and warned Otis to drop his weapon. Otis did as he was instructed and Ramon took that opportunity to snatch the knife previously held by Pam. He grabbed Zoe by the ankle and dragged her across the floor to him. By the time the cops pulled their weapons, Ramon had the knife to Zoe's throat.

"I swear to God I will slit her throat if y'all don't get out of here," Ramon warned as he positioned Zoe directly in front of him. He knew that if he used her as a shield the cops would never take a shot at him. "I keep telling y'all that all I want to do is talk. Once I say what I came to say, I'll let her go, but I won't do it with all of y'all in here."

"Take it easy," one cop instructed. "Things will go a lot easier for you if you put the knife down and come with us."

"Get out," Ramon shouted. "Get out or I will kill her right now!" he warned as he dug the knife into her throat just enough to draw blood. Zoe cried out in pain and fear.

Seeing the blood ooze from her daughter's neck made Martha beg the cops to back off. "Please do as he says, please… I don't want to see my daughter die," she sobbed. "Just give him what he wants and step away."

The cops backed out of the house slowly and Ramon ordered Otis to close the door. He stood to his feet pulling Zoe up with him. He ordered everyone to a back bedroom and warned them not to come out. He ushered Zoe back to the kitchen and instructed her to take a seat. She did as she was told all while offering up silent prayers for the safety of her and her family. "Zoe, why did you leave me?"

Zoe looked at him as if he were crazy. "Are you serious, you don't know why?"

"I know we had problems and I'm sorry that I let my anger take over, but I didn't do anything to warrant your leaving me like that. You shot out the door like you were some kind of runaway slave."

"Are you insane? You beat me like a dog and then held me on the floor and offered me up like a whore to your sick ass brother. What part of that is okay to you? Who do you think would stick around for that kind of treatment?"

"If you loved me you would've stayed. That's what real love is about, staying through the good and bad. I wasn't really gonna let you perform oral on Rich. I was just screwing with you and you should've known that." The entire time Ramon talked he twirled the point of the knife around on Zoe's thigh. The blood from his cut hand and her thigh mingled together into a puddle on the floor.

"That is not real love, Ramon. You don't hurt the people you love, you don't screw around with them like that. If you really loved me you wouldn't be cutting up my leg right now," Zoe said as she tried to steady her voice and hold back tears. "Ramon, you need help."

"I don't need no damn help!" he shouted as he pushed the knife deeper into Zoe's leg. Her painful cries made him realize what he was doing. He pulled the knife out of her leg as he offered up apologies. "Oh baby, I didn't mean to do that. Does it hurt? You want me to get some alcohol?"

"No! No baby, I don't want any alcohol. It'll be okay," she cried. Then the flashing lights caught Zoe's attention. There were obviously a ton more cop cars outside and she thought maybe she could use their presence to reason with Ramon. "Baby, look outside, do you see all those lights? It must be a bunch of cops out there. The longer you keep me in here the worse it'll be for you later. We've had a chance to talk now and I can admit my wrong. I shouldn't have run out on you like that, but I was scared. Not scared of you but of Rich, he doesn't love me like you do. I promise that if we go out together, I'll stick by your side through everything." She watched as Ramon peaked through the blinds and shook his head. She couldn't tell if he was confused or angry.

"They've got a fucking S.W.A.T truck out there! Why are they doing all this, all I wanted to do was talk to you. I mean damn, can't couples talk in peace anymore?"

Zoe now understood that he had mentally checked out. For him not to understand that he was holding a house full of hostages or think that this forced conversation was okay was a clear sign of insanity. It all made her more fearful that this situation would play out the same as the one between his parents had…with both of them dead.

"Let's just go out and let them know that we've just been talking and there's no need for all of this force." Zoe was hopeful that what she was saying was getting through because he dropped the knife in the sink. But suddenly a voice came blaring through a bullhorn causing Ramon to jump and grab his weapon.

"Ramon, this is Captain Owens, looks like you've caused quit a commotion out here. We can bring all this to an end if you'll put down your weapon and come out with your hands up."

"How the hell do they know my name?"

"I don't know baby," Zoe spoke slowly as she rose from her chair. "But let's just do like they said and walk out with our hands up." She gently took him by the hand and took a step towards the door.

Martha, Pam, and Otis had cracked the door to listen to all that was going on and was hopeful that Zoe had gotten through to Ramon. But when they heard Ramon yell, "Bitch, you're trying to set me up. I'm not going to jail!" and Zoe screamed when he slapped her across the face, their hopes quickly died.

"Do y'all have anything in here that can be used as a

weapon?" Otis asked as he desperately looked around the bedroom.

"I have a gun," Martha admitted. "But how can I trust you not to use it against us? How do we know that you didn't come here to kill us?" she cried.

"Martha, I've been here for weeks, I know where you all moved from, where you work, and I know when you moved here. If I wanted to hurt any of you I could've done so a long time ago. I swear I came here to make peace, to apologize. Now you can believe me or not, but the longer we stand here talking the more danger we're putting Zoe in. Where's the gun?"

Martha hesitantly went to retrieve the 9mm. She held the gun on Otis for a few minutes, but when they heard Zoe cry out again, she reluctantly handed him the gun.

Back in the kitchen, Ramon held Zoe in front of him and shouted from the window for the cops to back off or he'd kill everyone in the house. The captain continued to try and reason with him, but Ramon was now acting like a mad dog and had no intention of backing down. "If y'all don't leave by the time I count to three I'm going to cut this bitch's jugular!" he shouted as he poked the knife further into Zoe's neck. "1…2…" POP!

CHAPTER THIRTY-FOUR

The shot to the shoulder sent Ramon falling to the ground and provoked the S.W.A.T. Team to bust through the back door. Otis dropped the gun he'd used to shoot his daughters captor and Ramon was taken into custody and whisked off in an ambulance. Medics attended to Zoe and let her family know that she was being transported to Emory University Hospital for treatment of her wounds. Martha, Pam, and Otis stayed behind to answer all of the officer's questions. All Martha wanted to do was get to her daughter, but the questions seemed to go on forever. Finally, after about an hour's worth of explanations, they were permitted to go see about Zoe.

Against Pam's wishes, Martha allowed Otis to ride with them to the hospital. Martha thought that it was the least she could do and this would give Otis the chance to tell them all why he felt the need to stalk them. Pam opted to sit in the backseat so that she could have a clear view of Otis. He may have saved Zoe, but she still didn't trust anything about him. For Pam no matter what he did, he'd never be more than an evil monster. The ride was quiet and Pam's eye's never left her father. After a twenty minute ride they pulled into the hospital's parking garage and rushed to the information desk. "What room is Zoe Shaw in?" Martha asked anxiously.

"Take the elevator to the sixth floor and you'll find her in room 615," the desk clerk said.

They rushed to her room and both Martha and Pam breathed a sigh of relief when they saw Zoe sitting up sipping on some juice. Thankfully the cut on her neck was superficial and the one to her thigh only required ten stitches. Martha praised God that her baby was going to be alright.

"What is he doing here?" Zoe asked flatly.

"I let him come to see for himself that you were okay. I thought that we owed him that much since he saved your life," Martha confessed.

"Mama we don't owe him a damn thing!" Zoe snarled. "Now what are you doing here, Otis? What are you after?"

"I'm not after anything. I'm just here to see for myself that you're okay. I swear I didn't come to cause any trouble; my whole point in coming to Atlanta was to apologize to my girls and my wife. I've had nothing but time to think about all the ways I did you all wrong and I am so sorry. More sorry than you'll ever know."

"Okay, we've heard your apology. I thank you for saving my life, but we are no longer your girls and she is not your wife. That life is over and you have no claim on any of us. If you are as sorry as you claim to be, you'll leave Atlanta and leave us alone forever." Zoe was very cold, very matter-of-fact in all that she said.

"If that's what will make you girls happy then that's what I'll do. I'll be gone by the weekend," Otis promised.

"Yes, that's what will make all of us happy. There is no room for you in our lives and no part of either of us desires to have you around," Zoe declared.

"Do you feel the same way Martha?" Otis seemed to hold his breath as he waited for her answer.

"Yes, that's exactly how she feels," Zoe answered for her mother.

Pam stayed quiet the entire time. She never uttered a single word, never took her eyes off of Otis. And she held on to her purse for dear life. Zoe kept an eye on her sister, she was worried that Pam was about to become completely undone. But the longer she looked at Pam, the more she realized that Pam wasn't falling apart, but instead she was growing stronger, staying focused and in control.

"Mama, Zoe needs her rest and we need to get home. It's time to go," Pam instructed. "I love you Zoe and I'll check on you later." Pam kissed her sister on the cheek and Martha did the same.

"I love you baby. Get some rest and we'll see to you later," Martha whispered to her baby.

Outside the hospital, Otis asked if they could give him a ride back to his old truck that was still parked outside of their house. Again, against Pam's wishes Martha agreed and they all loaded back up in the car. The ride back was filled with Otis' attempts to convince Martha that he was a changed man. "I've never stopped loving you Martha," he said. "I've worked hard to become a better man. I even became a key part of the prison ministry. I got saved baby. I know The Lord now and He's changed my life."

"Well I'm happy for you Otis. Now take your new found relationship with God and rely on it to build a good life for yourself. Live positively this time, do something worthwhile," Martha encouraged.

"Martha I was thinking that since the girls are doing well now and that Ramon character is no longer a threat to Zoe, maybe you could come back with me. We could start all over. You know the way it was before we had the girls. We used to be good together, baby, used to have fun. What do you say, can we start over?"

Martha whipped the car into the drive, threw it in park, and stepped out. She stood there and looked at Otis as if he had two heads. "Otis there is no way I could or would ever go back to a life with you. I don't even want you in the same town as me let alone the same house. You need to go back home and work on building that positive life we just talked about."

Pam opened her car door but didn't get out. She sat listening to the exchange of words and wondered if Otis would take no for an answer and just leave. But the longer they talked the more she realized that he wouldn't go without putting up a fight.

"Baby don't you get it? I came back for you. All the changes I've made I made for you. My life will be so much better with you in it Martha. I know you still love me, don't you?"

"Absolutely not! You beat all the love I had for you right out of me. I have nothing for you now Otis, nothing at all."

"You don't mean that Martha, now come on and let's go," he said as he grabbed her by the hand. "There's no need to pack anything. We can get you anything you need once we get back home."

Martha snatched her hand away. "I am home Otis! Now you need to leave."

"Not without my wife. Now let's go," he said grabbing her hand again. But this time he held his grip and wouldn't let her pull away from him. "I know we can have a good life this time. I promise we will." Otis was damn near dragging Martha to his truck. She tried to free herself from him but her efforts were in vain. When she was finally able to land a punch and rip her arm free, he turned and punched her in the mouth. "You are coming with me, now get in the truck. Don't you understand? I won't live without my wife," he said as he started dragging her to the truck.

Pam reached in her purse and grabbed the gun she'd purchased after she first thought she'd seen Otis. She knew she wasn't crazy, that monster's face was one she could never forget. She jumped in front of Otis with the small caliber pistol drawn. "Let her go now!"

"Pam this has nothing to do with you, now put that thing away before someone gets hurt." Otis never released his grip on Martha. "Move girl, get out of the way!"

"I'm going to say it one more time, let her go."

"Damn it girl..." Otis lunged at Pam and without hesitation she pulled the trigger. But she didn't shoot to injure, Pam shot to kill and that's just what she did. Otis fell dead in the street just like the dog he was.

CHAPTER THIRTY-FIVE

The prison cells clinked and Rich and Ramon looked around at their new home. While Ramon was holding hostages, Rich was being held by the ladies of the women's shelter after they saw him attack Candy. They ganged up on him, beat him, and held him for the cops. And yes, the state pen was where they would both live out the next ten to fifteen years.

Meanwhile, on the other side of town, all of the food had been prepared, flowers placed, and the decorations were gorgeous. The back yard looked like the Garden of Eden. Martha, Zoe, and April ran around in their beautiful dresses making sure that everything and everyone was in place. The minister stood under the floral arch and the small trio of musicians started playing. Martha took her seat up front and then Zoe and April began their walk down the aisle. Zoe smiled as her eyes fell on both Alvin and Desi all dressed in their tuxes, looking so handsome and happy.

The wedding march started to play, signaling Pam and Kirk to begin their waltz down the aisle hand-in-hand. For Kirk and Desi, the ceremony was a grand gesture of their love and commitment, but for Pam and Alvin, it was all that and more, it was a marriage ceremony. After all the drama, Pam realized that there was no one that could comfort her and love her like Alvin. So she ran out, bought a band, and proposed to him. Now here they were, exchanging vows, promising to love, honor, protect, and respect each other all the days of their lives.

The celebration lasted long into the night with the guests eating, drinking, and dancing. Martha and Zoe stood back and watched as Pam danced with her husband. They shared her joy and were excited to know that they could all live free of fear. Never again could Otis or Ramon harm them. After Pam killed Otis, they worried about her state of mind and her freedom. But mentally she'd never been better. By Otis leaving the DC area, he was in violation of his probation. That coupled with the neighbors attesting to his attack on Martha, Pam was found to have been justified in the shooting.

Zoe felt a tap on the shoulder, spun around, and smiled broadly, "Candy! I'm so glad you could make it," she beamed.

"I wouldn't have missed it for the world. And Zoe, thank you for being my friend. After everything that happened, it would've been so easy for you to forget about me, never speak to me again. But you chose to stick by me, to help me get my life together, and I can't thank you enough."

"Trust me, you already have," Zoe said as she held Candy in a warm embrace. "Now go grab a bite to eat and let's dance the night away."

ACKNOWLEDGMENTS

Not everyone is able to recognize their God given talents.

I thank The Lord for blessing me with the gift of writing, allowing me to live out my dreams and surrounding me with supportive people. God is good to me!

Thank you, Kenneth and Joshua Lee for your support of my work, your patience with me and willingness to travel with me while I do this "writing thing." I love you both so dearly.

Thank you Mommy (Myrtice Covington) for your love and wisdom and for selling my books like no one else can. Last but certainly not least, I'd like to give a huge shout out to every reader, book club, interviewer, and reviewer that has ever read one of my books. The love and support you've shown me is incredible and it encourages me to be a better writer for us all. Thank you!

NATIONAL DOMESTIC VIOLENCE HOTLINE

Physical, mental, emotional, and/or financial abuse is never okay. If you or someone you love is being abused, please seek help.

Call the National Domestic Violence Hotline at 1-800-799-7233 or TTY 1-800-787-3224 to speak with an advocate or reach them online at www.thehotline.org.

Help is available!

ALSO BY BY STACEY COVINGTON-LEE

The Knife In My Back

The Knife In My Back 2

Bitter Taste Of Love

When Love Ain't Enough

The Love That Lies Between Us

Coming summer 2019, her much anticipated novel, He Won't Go.

For bookings please email inquires@staceycovingtonlee.com.

Made in the USA
Columbia, SC
13 December 2021